Also by Wayne Hixon

Vampires in Devil Town

To Those Who Know,

Shhhhh. Mystery is beautiful.

Bright Black Moon

Wayne Hixon

GRINDHOUSE PRESS

Published by Grindhouse Press
POB 292644
Dayton, OH 45429
www.grindhousepress.com

Bright Black Moon: Vampires in Devil Town Book Two
Grindhouse Press #008
ISBN-13: 978-0-9849692-1-0
ISBN-10: 0984969217

This book is a work of fiction.

Bright

Black

Moon

Ten Years Ago

"What's a Devil?"

Gloria looked down at John, only nine, snuggled into the covers of his racecar-shaped bed. She had just kissed his forehead and risen, ready to leave the room. The question caught her off-guard.

What was *a Devil?*

The boy had her attention.

She sat back down on the edge of the bed.

"Where did you hear about *them?*"

"Some kids at school. They said that's what got Elliot."

Just the thought of her oldest son, now dead, sent a cold shiver through Gloria. And that name, "the Devils," made her seethe. It reminded her of the fact that nothing—not a thing about the murder—had been resolved. The fact that it still, to this day, nearly two years later, had never been called a murder, did nothing to restore hope in Gloria. Because what could be worse than death? She didn't want to think about that. She didn't want to think of what might be happening to him. All those things worse than death. She almost wished they had found him with his throat slashed on the side of the road—a horrible thought, she knew— rather than thinking of what kind of torture he might still be undergoing. And if he were to be found alive, she knew he wouldn't be the Elliot she had mothered for all those years. He would be someone else.

So one of the only comforts she had was that, looking at John, she knew he was safe and sound. But just hearing that word in his mouth made her want to reach her hands down his throat and pull it back out. Or maybe reach into his brain and erase that knowledge. It was like he was tainted.

And Gloria didn't have the first clue how to answer him.

She ran her fingers through his short brown hair and said, "You can't believe everything the kids at school say."

"I know."

"I know you know, honey. You're a good kid. A smart kid and me and daddy love you very much."

"But..."

"But what?"

John shifted uncomfortably. "I still want to know what they are."

"They're made-up, buddy."

"I know that but, well, lots of things are made-up. Like vampires and werewolves and stuff are all made up but you still know what they *are*. Like *the* Devil... Well, he might not be made up... Are they like him?"

"Stay around here long enough and you'll find out what they are. For now, imagine the worst possible monsters you can— vampires, werewolves, demons, zombies, whatever—and then roll them all up into one... Can you imagine that?"

Gloria watched as, wide-eyed, John nodded his head. She didn't know what brought on this sudden burst of near sadism. "Okay," she said. *"That's* a Devil."

Slowly, nervously, John shut his eyes, almost like he was expecting the nightmare waiting behind them. Gloria put her hand on his shoulder.

"And you know what?" she said. "There is absolutely no such

thing as a Devil. Maybe not even *the* Devil."

John opened his eyes and said, "Can I sleep with you and Dad tonight?"

"Big boys don't sleep with their parents."

"I know. I miss Elliot."

"We all miss Elliot. And we're all a little scared but you still have to sleep in your own bed. Your dad and me are right down the hall if you need us. Okay?"

"Okay."

"Good night, big guy."

She kissed him on the forehead and exited the room, leaving the door cracked far enough to filter an ample amount of light from the hallway.

She felt bad about not letting John sleep with her and Gordon. She would have let him but then he would hear her screaming. Or Gordon screaming. That, she thought, would be more realistically terrifying than whatever natural nightmares he had from losing his brother. Those would fade in the dawn, maybe left to linger somewhere in the subconscious. But the last thing little John needed was the sound of his full-grown parents, one of whom had just told him the Devils didn't exist, screaming through his ears and viscera. That, Gloria thought, would not fade with the morning. That would generate questions. One of those questions would inevitably be, "What was the nightmare about?" And then she would have to tell him. And that might make him even more infected than he already was.

She opened the door to her bedroom and Gordon said, "I left the light on for you."

She chuckled. It was their little joke.

They left the light on every night.

One

The storm hadn't come yet.

Later, when John Fresk tried to figure out why some memories were sunlit, yellow things and others were black, red, swollen and painful, he would think of that phrase: *The storm hadn't come yet*.

Much like the disappearance of his brother, the storm changed everything.

Two

It was early June and John could not even contemplate registering for classes at the community college in Dayton. This would be his second year out of high school and there was a part of him that wanted to do something besides sulk around the house but, in the end, he just couldn't imagine doing it.

It wasn't that he had an aversion to schoolwork. On the contrary, when in school, he had done quite well. His aversion lay mainly with school itself. He just couldn't seem to shake the memories of Lynchville High and the student body populating its grimly fluorescent hallways.

He had been a product of that school system since kindergarten and had managed to avoid making a single friend. He couldn't imagine why some low-rent local community college would be any different. He had no idea why, exactly. He didn't stand out in any way. He wasn't unfriendly. He wasn't exceptionally ugly. The only thing he could really pin it on was his intense shyness. If a teacher asked him a question, his face turned red. Group work made him physically ill. If they ever planned a field trip, he was sure to miss that day. Therefore, since he wasn't charismatic enough for people to approach *him*, there really wasn't any contact with other students. On the few occasions when it was forced, his throat closed up, his brain shut down, and he could only mumble with extreme brevity if anybody ever asked him a question.

In a small school like Lynchville, it didn't take long for his shyness to be intrinsically felt. Eventually, even in group work, eyes glanced over him, knowing he wouldn't do anything except mumble, "I don't know," and look down at the desk in front of him. He became unacknowledged, invisible. For the most part, he was pretty sure people avoided him and had avoided him ever since Elliot disappeared. Sometimes John felt like this was because people saw him as, somehow, the cause of the horrible crime or, at the very least, *symbolic* of the crime. Either that or the other students saw him as being cloaked in some kind of all-pervasive sadness. If at all possible, most children avoided "downers."

Maybe he just came off as being incredibly rude. By the time he graduated he felt like he didn't know anything.

Since graduating, he often wondered if school had been the only thing that brought this particular affliction on or if he simply no longer had anything to gauge it against. When speaking with teachers on a one-to-one basis, he didn't have any problems— some of them even found him extremely bright—a complete opposite of the stammering half-wit who couldn't answer the simplest of questions when surrounded by a sea of fellow pimply faces.

At family functions, even though most of the people there were more or less strangers, he did not have any problems talking with them. He had even managed to kiss his cousin, LeAnn, at the last reunion he had attended nearly three years ago. Never mind how his face had burned red with embarrassment when they retreated from the woods and back into the folds of their family, every adult eye accusatory. *You actually kissed your cousin*, had been his later thought. And this wasn't a second or third cousin, either. This was his mom's niece.

He made it a point to avoid her on future occasions. He had

been a virgin at the time. He was, in fact, still a virgin. He had no doubt he would do whatever she asked him to do. It pained him to ever have to admit he lost his virginity to his cousin. After all, that's really what she had wanted and there were times, lying in bed at night, when he kicked himself for not trying to go further with her.

College will be different. That was the mantra that got him out of bed in the morning. *Maybe I should just go off to a college, some place far away, and reinvent myself. I could become a regular Mr. Congeniality.* He chuckled at the thought.

Now, sitting in the kitchen of the old farmhouse, eating dinner with his mother and father, the last day of high school nearly a full year behind him, things didn't seem so bad. Or maybe he had just gotten used to whatever depression had taken root in his brain, leaving him to comfortably muddle through his days.

"Do you have any plans for this summer?" his mom asked.

"Not really. Probably get a lot of reading done. Maybe pick out my college." Sometimes he hated being an only child. It made him the focal point of all his parents' attention. The idea of college was the only thing that really held them off. He didn't know how long he would be able to dangle that in front of them.

"Are you going to stay in state?" his mother asked. They continued to humor him.

"I don't know yet. I might just go to Sinclair."

"You know," his father said. "It costs about double if you want to go someplace out of state."

His father always thought about money. This was another reason why John wasn't so sure of how long he could go without working or attending school.

"Yeah, I know. That's why I said I'd probably go to Sinclair. It's like twenty minutes away. I'd probably be working."

"You think about getting a job this summer?"

"Not really. I don't think there are any places around here to work. I have the rest of my life to work."

He was almost certain that would goad his father into saying something. Instead, there was just a long, uncomfortable silence. These silences were as common as food around the dinner table.

"You could at least look," his father finally said.

"I have," John answered. "Have you bothered checking out the classifieds in the paper? There aren't really a whole lot of jobs in there. And there's not much about Lynchville online at all."

Before his father could say anything else, his mother came to the rescue.

"Have you looked at any scholarships?"

John lied and told her he had missed the deadlines for this year. His parents continued their battery of questions around quiet bites of meatloaf and mashed potatoes. John felt his muscles tightening. His answers became more and more succinct. The less information he gave them, the less they had to feed from. Eventually, their conversation drifted into the harmless banality of every evening. His mother talked about her day at the local bank. His father talked about his work at the nature reserve. John was usually silent during these conversations. What could he say that would bring his general malaise into even sharper focus? "Oh, yeah, today I slept until two or so, got up, watched some TV. Read a little bit. I mean, I picked up the phone to call a couple of colleges but realized I couldn't say anything when they answered."

After dinner, he went outside. The farmhouse was relatively large for a family of three but with its low ceilings, thick stone walls, and lack of central air conditioning, he often felt oppressed by it. The fact that, when the house was purchased, it was intended for four, made it even more oppressive. Outside, on warm summer nights, he got a taste of what he hoped would be the freedom of college if he could only muster up the energy or desire or whatever to go. They had a large barn once used for cattle and storage that he ducked into whenever it rained.

This evening was clear. The sun, sinking down toward the horizon in front of the house, warmed him. Everything looked and sounded alive. Way off in the distance he heard lawnmowers and the barking of dogs. Cicadas rattled their hollow-bodied moan. Birds chirped. The wind periodically gathered itself up into a gust, only to be sleepily caught by the trees. The corn in the fields grew up just over a foot.

He was currently reading a curious book called *Vampires in Devil Town* by a writer named Wayne Hixon. It looked like it was his first book. He tucked the book under his arm and walked slowly across the gravel driveway and over to the open, uncultivated field. A mown path led from the driveway over to the pond. Grasshoppers bounced over the path in front of him. Butterflies fluttered lazily before speeding off and out of sight. Once at the pond, he sat down on a small bench his father had put there as an anniversary gift to his mother and started on his book. The rubber band sounds of the little frogs, the hoarse groan of the bullfrogs and the muddy splashing of their restlessness slowly faded away as John lost himself to the words on the pages.

Three

The next two weeks continued like that. Throughout the day, while his parents were at work, he stayed in the house, scrounging up things to eat and watching television, a noisy box fan crammed in the window three feet beside his bed. Sometimes he would delve into the modest porno collection his parents kept in the television stand in their room. He figured if he did have a girlfriend, or friends of any kind really, they could busy themselves with all kinds of vice. Never mind that his friends would probably have jobs or be away at school or something. He read *Vampires in Devil Town* three more times.

The local noon news on Channel 45 said there was a storm system moving rapidly into the area, probably to hit around six or so. Thus far, the doughy anchorman said, this system had been characterized by large hail, heavy winds, and torrential rains. He ominously noted that several funnel clouds had been spotted. Then they showed scenes of damage in western Indiana.

John couldn't wait. He loved thunderstorms. The front porch faced west and it was always an awesome spectacle to watch the storms come in from way off on the horizon.

He got a can of Pepsi out of the refrigerator and took it out to the front porch. Already the wind had picked up from that morning. It wouldn't be long before there was an electric chill to it. He finished his Pepsi and went upstairs to take a nap, preceded by a quick masturbation session. He found he masturbated at least once a day and didn't feel the slightest bit guilty about it.

Four

John woke up suddenly. He had the feeling he'd overslept for something. The wind had picked up. It rushed against his box fan, speeding it up, the cool air chilling him. Earlier, before pleasuring himself, he'd stripped off his shirt so he didn't sweat all over it. Now his sweat had dried and he grabbed for his discarded t-shirt, black with a pocket over the left breast. He always insisted his t-shirts have a pocket. Part of the reason for this, he guessed, was that he always had the idea he would start carrying a notebook and begin jotting down the stories running through his head. Thus far, he'd never done that.

He unlocked his door and went downstairs, surprised to hear his mother banging around in the kitchen. That meant it was after five.

"Hey there," she said when she saw him. "You been asleep?"

"Yeah."

"Garlic chicken sound okay for dinner?"

"Sure," John mumbled, grinding the heel of his hand into sleep-sanded eyes. "Dad home yet?"

"No, but he called a few minutes ago. He should be home soon. Looks like there's a bad storm on the way. He's figuring he'll probably have to go out later."

"Yeah, I saw it on the news. Tore up a bunch of stuff in Indiana."

"I heard that too. The weatherman on the radio said it's gaining speed as it moves this way. They've put all of southwestern Ohio under a tornado watch."

"Guess we can always hide in the cellar, huh?"

"As disgusting as that may be."

The cellar had a tendency to flood and there was usually a half a foot of stagnant water in it at any given time. Along with the outhouse, it was one of the family's running jokes. Many times, John had sarcastically been threatened with the cellar as punishment.

His mother pulled a chicken out of the refrigerator, removed it from its plastic container, and plopped it into an aluminum foil-lined pan. She put the pan in the oven just as Gordon Fresk came through the door smelling like cigarettes and outside, his thin hair tousled around the top of his head. "Jesus, it's windy out there," he said. "It's gonna be a good one."

"You think?" John asked with maybe a little bit of hope in his voice.

"It'll probably be on us in about a half an hour."

"I think I'm gonna go over by the pond while there's time."

"Be careful," his mother said.

It seemed like she made a point to tell him to be careful every time he stepped out the door, regardless of where he went. Regardless of how old he was. One of the other perks of being an adult child, he figured.

Christ, he thought. *I'm just walking over to the pond.* Usually he said it out loud. This time he did not. He simply nodded, as though taking her words into consideration, and walked out the front door.

Five

The bench by the pond faced east, so John sat down on the grass behind it and leaned his head against it. Out over the horizon he watched the storm clouds—black, gray and billowy, churning over and over on themselves. Forming a distinct line, they contrasted sharply with the blue sky immediately overhead, looking like it would become a thing of the past.

He sat and relished the feel of the cool clean air brushing over his skin. The wind would pause before rushing toward him again, bending the tops of the trees, collectively rustling their leaves with a sleepy wash of sound.

Yeah, it was going to be a big one.

Part of the reason he loved these storms so much was because of the energy he seemed to suck from them. The storm charged toward him, a jagged bolt of lightning coming out of those clouds like a hand from the grave. It was a powerful energy. The moments before a storm, he felt like he could do anything. Shivers danced across his skin and in his bones, shooting up and down his spine. Then the rain would come and he would have to retreat into the house, trapped in that day's captured warmth.

But what if he didn't go inside?

What if he decided to stay out here in the storm? Out here where the lightning did a neon skeleton's dance and the rain attempted to beat the earth into submission.

Would he be able to take away a little bit of that power? Retain it?

It looked like he would soon get his chance to find out. The storm came up quickly and, with the first drops of icy cold rain on his skin, his mind was made up.

He stood, elation widening his eyes and quickening his pulse. The storm put a spring in his step and, running through the field, the grass whipping around his shins, he rushed to meet it.

Six

Cassie looked over at Gregory, gelatinously situated in the driver's seat, and once again cursed her fate.

He was in one of his moods again. They'd left the school over an hour ago and Gregory had forced her to become his companion as he swung his Mustang around Lynchville's twisty back roads.

When she thought of Gregory, the word 'oxen' came to mind. His head was large, indiscernible from his neck. He kept his hair in a burr cut and his eyebrows crept toward each other, trying desperately to become one. Fate and her parents were the only reasons Cassie was in the car with Gregory. It was always 'Gregory' and never 'Greg,' like he hadn't quite grown up yet. He certainly looked like an overgrown child. Cassie could imagine ice cream or drool clinging to his chin in place of the festering zits currently inhabiting that terrain. She was surprised people didn't still call him 'Greggy,' for that's who he always reminded her of. The fat little boy who had locked her in the closet and wouldn't let her come out unless she showed him her underwear.

Gregory lived down Maple Street from her. They were two of only like five kids from Lynchville who went to Saint Agnes, the Catholic school in Milltown, and it seemed to be the absolute *last* school to get out for the summer. She had Latin Club after school and Gregory tutored an underclassman, probably just so he could have an excuse to be there to take her home. She had grown up with Gregory and didn't know how to tell her parents he had become the creepy boy in the neighborhood and she didn't really want to be seen with him. And he wasn't creepy in a cool way like some of the geeks she knew. No, Gregory was creepy in the sense that it wasn't hard to imagine him keeping children tied up in the shed out behind his house.

She thought Gregory was about ready to head home when he pulled his car off Creek Road and into the lot overlooking the Saints River and the Lynchville dam. Sometimes Gregory did this and she would sit uncomfortably and listen while he either ranted about his parents or asked her if she knew if so and so liked him.

He turned the car off and the air conditioning went with it. She started to roll down her window until she realized they were automatic. Gregory rested his plump hands nervously on his khaki-covered thighs, part of St. Agnes's school uniform for males, and looked cluelessly out toward the river.

"We should probably try and get home," she said. "I think there's a big storm on the way."

She waited for some type of response from him but he delayed in giving it. Finally, he said, "You know, Cassie, I think you're really hot and was thinking, if you don't have a boyfriend or anything, maybe we could see each other."

The car was already stiflingly hot.

"Do you think you can turn the car on so I can roll down my window?"

"Did you hear me, Cassie?"

"Gregory... This... Well, this is kind of out of the blue, isn't it? I mean, we don't *really* even know each other." An uncomfortable dampening started at her armpits. She felt claustrophobic.

"But I feel like I know you better than just about anyone. You're the only girl I ever hardly talk to."

She pushed a strand of black hair behind her ear and adjusted her plaid skirt, trying to pull it as far down on her knees as she could. She suddenly felt too exposed.

"What I mean is that I don't know if we would have a lot in common. Maybe if you talked to more girls, you would find one you really enjoyed talking to."

"But I like talking to you a lot. We could have things in common. I'd go anywhere you wanted me to go. I'd listen to the music you wanted to listen to. Do the things you wanted to do."

For a moment, she was sort of stunned. He looked like he was getting ready to cry, staring out over the river, his bottom lip twitching.

She reached over and patted him on the shoulder and said, "I just don't think it would work."

He shrugged her hand off.

"You're not seein anybody, are you?"

"Well, no."

"Then why not?"

She breathed in a damp mouthful of nuclear hot air and willed the questions to go away. She was trying really hard not to get mad. However much of a beast Gregory was, the poor boy didn't deserve to hear what she actually thought about him.

"Have you ever had sex with anybody?" He looked straight at her now, his face red, sweat beading up and rolling down out of his caramel-colored hairline.

She had had sex with one boy. He went to public high school in a neighboring and much larger town. They'd met at a mall around Dayton. One of the reasons she decided to make him her first was because she knew she wouldn't have to deal with the embarrassment at school the next day, the other boys with their tongues lolling out, the girls who would look at her like a slut. She didn't even tell any of her friends about him. It was really just something she wanted to get over with—to experience. She had been fifteen at the time. That was late last summer. They had, over the course of a month, made love four times. The last time she had seen him was when he dropped her off at her house after picking her up from the abortion clinic. She hadn't felt any particular craving for sex since.

She didn't know what to tell Gregory. *Why not just be honest?* she thought.

"Yeah."

"Well I haven't. And I'm almost two years older than you."

"That's okay. I wish I had never had it in the first place."

The car was like a sauna, the sweat flowing freely from both of them now.

He put a heavy hand on her left thigh.

"We don't have to be boyfriend and girlfriend. Just… just let me kiss you and I won't bother you again, I swear."

"I'm not like that. I'm sorry."

"But you already told me you were like that."

"I think you got it wrong. I was taken advantage of by an older boy. Someone who shouldn't have been messing with a girl my age. Someone like you."

"Just give me something, Cassie. Touch me or let me see your tits or your pussy or something. Come on, I'll show you mine."

Before she could stop him, he unzipped his pants and pulled his penis from the opening of his boxers.

She looked away.

"Come on, look."

"Gregory, you're scaring me."

"Is it big enough for you? Feel it." He grabbed her left hand and folded it around his stiff penis. She tried to pull it away. God, the heat took the life away from her muscles. She felt his beginning wetness on the back of her hand.

Jaws clenched, she said, "Take me home."

He let go of her hand and put his left hand over her chest, clumsily, battling his girth.

She finally opened her eyes, feeling like it was a matter of survival. He had turned toward her, one of his knees up on the driver's seat. She tried to scoot away from his hand, but this put her back against the door and her lap toward him.

"What the hell are you doing?" Cassie panicked. Her whole body shook. She didn't like the look in his eyes. His right hand stroked his dick. His pants were gathered beneath his hairy scrotum.

Maybe he'll just come all over me and that'll be it, she thought.

Then he took his hand away from his dick and shoved her skirt up above her panties. With his left hand, he tore at her shirt, popping the first few buttons, tugging her bra down so the nipples were over top of it.

"Oh God, Gregory, are you *raping* me?"

She kept trying to back away from him but fear and heat were really fucking with her head. And there was that door she kept backing up against. The handle digging into her back was the only thing preventing her shirt from getting completely ripped off.

He tugged at her underwear. She fought to keep her legs together but it just made it easier for him to drag her lower half across the rest of the car, the console digging into her ass. Unable to get the underwear down past her crotch, he put both hands in between her legs and tried to pry them apart. He was much stronger than she was but she started to get some of her thought processes back.

If she could just keep her legs closed for a few more seconds. She reached her left hand out to his penis, stroking it, trying to get him to pop before he could force her legs apart. The thought of it sent fingers of nausea through her stomach. But maybe, if he did that, he would lose interest. Touching him like that fueled her anger. If she thought she could, she would have ripped his whole cock off.

With her right hand, she reached into her backpack, sitting on the passenger-side floorboard, and enclosed her hand around the only book in there—Wayne Hixon's *Vampires in Devil Town*.

Now she took her hand off his cock and leaned forward like she wanted to kiss him, turning to put her arm on the door's armrest, conveniently below the handle.

He leaned in for a taste of her lips and she brought the book up, smashing it into the side of his head, trying to blow out an eardrum. Immediately, she grabbed the handle with her left hand, pulled it, and lunged out the door.

She threw her elbows out to stop her fall and they scraped painfully on the cement.

He grabbed her bunched up underwear and yanked them down so her ass was fully exposed to him. He grabbed her around the right calf. She imagined he was using his other hand to steady himself. Luckily, the only thing the school said about footwear was that the shoes had to be black. So Cassie rammed the heavy steel-toed combat boot on her left foot into the space where she thought Gregory's head would be. She felt it connect and then felt the thin bone of his nose collapse.

Right now the only thing she wanted to do was get away from him but he didn't drop his grip. If he got that bulk on her, she was gone for sure. And now, with everything she'd done to him, she thought she would probably get the raping of a lifetime.

He twisted her legs around so she was once again looking into the car. The first drops of rain came down all around them.

He scrambled across the car, projecting himself out and onto her.

If he's a virgin, she thought, *he'll be lucky to find the hole.*

He tried without lifting his torso off, smothering her. She noted the confusion on his face as she fought to close her legs and scoot back on the cement.

The rain began in earnest and it was deafening—huge fat drops splashing down.

He got up on his knees, holding her leather-clad ankles together with one hand and using the other to probe her sex for the opening. She rocked back, bringing her knees into her chest and maybe giving him just the briefest glimpse of what he searched so desperately for before driving both heels of her boots into his face, into his eye sockets.

Thunder sang metallic as his tenebrous grip fell away and she was off, running up into the nature reserve. If he could still see, she didn't want him able to find her.

She still had that book in her hand.

Seven

Twenty years of working in the Lynchville nature reserve and Dan Wrigley had never seen anything like this. He expected a little bit of craziness. Whenever a storm blew up, there were always a *few* moments of craziness. A few moments when he looked around at everything blowing—limbs, leaves, stuff coming out of the woods he didn't think was possible. Just a few moments where he had to think about the truly awesome spectacle nature was about to present. And maybe, somewhere in those few moments, there was a little bit of fear. He wondered just how bad things could get. He always expected the occasional tree down, maybe some flooding, maybe an accident to report. But tornadoes were not unknown around these parts and that was always something that kept him a little on edge.

But what he looked at right now made him feel downright creepy. An eeriness spread through his skin. It was eerie and somehow beautiful and amazing all at the same time.

He almost wished he hadn't let Gordon go home just so someone could back him up in what he was actually seeing. But Gordon had wanted to get home. It was Friday and Gordon was getting ready to spend one of his weeks of vacation he had earned and Dan didn't want to be the bastard and make him stay through this, even though he knew it would just be more shit he would have to deal with later.

Once Dan was certain it was going to storm, he took the Ford Ranger through the McDonald's on the state route to get some coffee. He figured he would just drive back to the ranger station, smoke his pipe, drink his coffee, and watch the storm unfold around him, waiting for the calls to come in. While waiting for his coffee, he packed his pipe and took the first couple of drags from it, relishing the cavendish aroma filling the cab of the truck. After getting his coffee, he took off toward the ranger station.

The rain started, light and then hard and then hammering.

Dan nervously twisted his mustache, took a pacifying drag from his pipe, turned the wipers on the highest setting, and continued on. He drove slowly. He waited for the day when a tree would come down on the road in front of him. He figured if he was going to be in the wrong place at the wrong time, it would be better if the tree came down in front of him rather than on the truck. There were some huge trees in the reserve, some of the largest documented trees in the county, and he didn't know how well the truck could hold one of them up. Anyway, if a tree came down in the road, he didn't want to be the one running into it.

The rain hammered down and when it switched to hail it drowned out the Stones playing on the classic rock station.

He slowed the truck to a crawl, nearly stopping.

From bad to worse, he thought. *Let's just hope this is as bad as it gets.*

And it wasn't really that it got any worse. Just, hell, he didn't know, it just got freaky.

The heavy clouds were overhead and it was almost like nighttime dark. Thunder roared. Lightning flashed, painfully bright. He watched the hail bounce off the hood of the truck and, farther in front of him, he saw something he knew was bound to stick in his memory for a very long time.

Crossing the road in front of him was some kind of mass

wildlife exodus.

This was what he had heard animals did during an earthquake or some shit like that. It was like they were all hurrying to get the hell away from something and quick. A herd of deer galloped across the road, into the woods on the other side, bounding frantically across the asphalt. The deer weren't everything though. There were raccoons and squirrels and chipmunks, the occasional dog or cat and, slithering across the asphalt—Dan could swear he saw them— all kinds of snakes. Garter snakes, black snakes, water snakes, corn snakes—so many of them, twisting and writhing around one another but all in a hurry to get away from whatever the hell was in the woods.

He sat in the cab of the stopped truck, hail pelting down, absently sucking on his pipe as he watched all the wildlife evacuate. They seemed to be coming from roughly the direction of the ranger station. He felt a brief pang of worry about Gordon and his family. They lived over that way and Dan didn't know what the fuck was happening at this point.

He was spooked.

Gooseflesh rippled his skin.

By the time the image of all of those animals crossing the road at the same time finally sank in, they were gone, lost in the foliage, rain, and hail. Somewhere on the other side of the road.

Where it's safer, he thought. *Where it's safer.*

He put the Ranger back in gear and started back toward the station, hoping that bit of strangeness would be the end of it.

The roads were already a mess with twigs and leaves. He would have to go out later and thoroughly drive through every area of the reserve. That was when the coffee would be worthwhile. Right now, all he could really think about doing was getting back to the ranger station to try and process the oddness he had just witnessed. He was already starting to doubt himself. Maybe he hadn't seen it at all. Whoever hears of that kind of thing happening? And he had been in the business for a long time, had heard just about every crazy story a person in a particular profession could hear. He had heard about devil worshippers and animal sacrifices, dead bodies, marijuana crops, people having sex on the trails, crazy people living in the reserve, the fucking Devils—but he had never heard about what he had just seen. What he *thought* he had just seen.

By the time he got to the ranger station, he was shaking. He didn't know why what he had seen should have a violent effect on him but it seemed to be having that effect anyway. He just wanted to get out of the truck and into the station. Luckily, the hail had stopped. He held the bowl of his pipe in the curve of his index finger and thumb, using the other three fingers to open the door. He held his cup of coffee in his right hand and silently cursed his girth as he slowly slid from the cab of the truck.

He was a big, tall man and took the few steps to the door of the station as quickly as a man of his size could. Still, it was raining so hard that by the time he actually unlocked the door and walked inside, he was soaked. Now, on his wet skin, the air conditioning that had seemed so nice earlier made him uncomfortably cold. He sat his coffee down on the desk butting up against the wall to the right of the door, crossed the dully tiled floor of the station and turned the thermostat off. He went back to the desk and, leaning over it, opened the large window above it.

He wheeled the ancient, battered chair out from beneath the desk and sat down in it. Reaching to his left, he flipped on the radio. It was set to the same classic rock station the radio in the truck was normally set to. The DJ announced it was time to get the Led out. They had reached the point of the day where they would play three Led Zeppelin songs in a row. One thing about the classic rock station was that it never changed.

His pipe had went out so he pulled his box of matches from his damp uniform breast pocket, struck one, and touched it to the bowl, puffing until it once again billowed smoke. He took a sip of his coffee and stared at the rain beating down.

Then he heard the boom.

Dan jerked.

The lid flew off the paper coffee cup and some of the scalding beverage landed on his gut.

With the boom, the inside of the station lit up. He didn't think that was supposed to happen. Maybe he just never really paid attention before but he couldn't recall thunder and lightning ever happening at the same time. Of course, that was assuming the boom was thunder and the flash was lightning.

What the fuck is happening?

If it was thunder, it was the loudest thunder he had ever heard. And if the flash had been lightning then it was the brightest flash of lightning he had ever seen. He grabbed the remote control to the TV off the desk and swiveled the chair around so it faced the 13-inch TV/VCR combo perched atop the filing cabinet across the station. He turned the TV to one of the more reliable stations. Sure enough, there was a tornado warning covering many of the counties in the left hand corner of the TV.

He had another idea about the flash and boom. It was entirely possible lightning had struck some kind of transformer or something, exploding it. That could have been what caused the boom. But if it had hit any kind of transformer nearby, then the generator would have taken over.

He retired his pipe to the ashtray on the desk and took another sip of his coffee.

The rain had lessened somewhat, the thunder already sounding like it was rolling away to the east. He took his coffee and wandered outside the ranger station.

The clouds were still dark overhead and even darker clouds were coming in from the west. He walked around the ranger station and looked northeast, toward Gordon's house. You could almost see it from the station but, during summer, there were just too many trees. Dan certainly didn't expect to see what he did.

Over in that direction, in an area encompassing maybe a half-mile, there was a rippling purple light. He couldn't tell if it came from the sky or the ground. Much like all the animals crossing the road, it was both eerie and beautiful at the same time.

After standing and staring at the unwavering intensity of the light, he went back into the station to call his wife and tell her it was probably going to be a long night, not to wait up, and to keep her eyes on the television. By the time he went back outside to look at the strange light, it was already gone and he thought it must have just been a trick of the sun and the rain.

Eight

With the first burst of hail, John decided staying out in the storm wasn't the best idea. Luckily, the hail didn't seem to be very large. It created a cacophony as it drummed down on his head. He put his arms together, hugging his crown, and ran for the barn.

He was all the way down by the road and the barn seemed far away, even with the wind at his back.

I can make it, he told himself. *It's just a thunderstorm.*

The hail died down and gave way to fat raindrops that, with the wind, were nearly as brutal. The rain continued to cut through his clothes, drilling against his skin. He tripped over a tight lump of grass and went sprawling face-first in the field.

That's when he noticed the sound.

He had often heard it said that a tornado sounds like a train. This didn't sound like a train. That didn't mean this wasn't a tornado.

The sound was loud and rumbly, overtaking the natural sounds of the storm like the wind and the rain beating down all around him. And there was something remotely *fleshy* about this sound, like it could have come from a human throat. A really huge human throat.

He scrambled to his feet and resumed running. He started to worry. It didn't seem like he had closed any difference between himself and the barn. He searched for the barn but found himself surrounded by a thick darkness. Lightning flashed, affording him a glimpse of the barn, silhouetted black against the purple bruise of the sky. He oriented himself. He was over near the driveway, a tall line of old oaks to his left, the wind whipping their canopies at nearly right angles to the ground.

This is bad, he thought.

The lightning dissipated and that roar was all around him again, scraping through his head and forcing him to move faster. He heard a loud cracking sound before being smashed by one of the dead branches from the oak tree. It smacked him in the head and then went skipping off across the field.

But he didn't see that.

He lay collapsed on the ground, still amazingly conscious, his hands held against the extreme pain blossoming on the back of his head.

This is even worse.

Now he no longer thought about getting to the barn. He just wanted to get to his feet and found that to be incredibly difficult. It was like the air around him was heavy and leaden.

He struggled to his knees before being quickly forced down on his back. The lightning beat the sky and he took in the depth of those black clouds rolling overhead. There wasn't even a speck of light on the horizon. No cessation in sight.

"Shit," he mumbled to himself.

His back was not the ideal place to be. There was too much valuable stuff on his front side for another branch, maybe a larger one, to bust up. What if the roof flew off the barn and came at him? He recoiled at the thought of rusty tin slicing through his skin.

He rolled back over onto his front and once again tried to stand up. This time the wind caught him, turning him over and over, hurling him in the direction of the pond.

Jesus, maybe it is *a fucking tornado.*

But there weren't really any signs of that. Keeping his eyes open, he could still see the rain around him when the lightning lit it up. He could see the ground below him. Nevertheless, he felt himself going round and round, a sickening, disorienting nausea growing in his stomach. Not to mention crippling fear.

The wind lifted him up until he guessed he was maybe about eight feet off the ground. The sound growled all around him and rumbled through his bones. Then the wind shifted, driving him into the ground. He came down primarily on his hip, but the shock ripped through every part of his body.

Crazy, but he began to think maybe it wasn't the wind moving him, but something else. Some other force. Cosmic puppet strings or something.

He struggled across the marshy grass, dragging himself by his elbows. He was once again over by the pond. Grateful he hadn't come down on the iron and wood bench, he decided to stay here, his arms over his head, his back to the raging rain and flying debris.

The lightning flashed across the black water of the pond. The cattails were broken. The creek willows did an insane dance directed at the sky. And there was something else. Something wasn't right because, when the lightning went away, the pond still glowed a blackish blue. And he thought about something he hadn't thought about for a very long time.

The Devils.

He had spent years trying to forget about them, whoever they were. Had even read *Vampires in Devil Town* four times without making the now obvious connection. And now he thought about them again, thought about them in something other than the context of a work of fiction, and didn't feel the extreme fear he had when he was a boy shivering in his bed and convincing himself it wasn't the sound of his parents' screaming that had woken him up. What he felt now was anger. He was angry about everything and, briefly, he felt whatever gray fog enshrouding him lift away. If there was a mystery, if there were such things as the Devils, he wanted to find out what it was and who they were.

He dragged himself to the edge and looked into the pond. Its water spiraled in a clockwise fashion. He had heard of waterspouts but he thought those were usually over larger bodies of water and this was spiraling down *into* the pond.

The movement and depression were punctuated with a muddy sucking sound.

Down into the heart of the mystery? he wondered.

Down and down the pond continued to delve, way past any possible depths it could actually contain.

Suddenly, he wanted to be away from the pond, but he knew it would be useless if he tried to run. So he lay there, watching the water tunnel continue to reach and reach. Maybe it was going to some other dimension.

The storm ceased to exist in his mind. There was only the pond and its unplumbed depths, reaching down toward some mystery he thought maybe he could find the answer to. It occurred to him that if he could not find the answer to this mystery then his life would be ruined. And what good would it be to continue living a ruined life?

He took a deep breath and stuck his head and torso out over the pond.

A heartbeat later, something came blazing out of the pond. He was thrown back with a blast of heat and a spray of water. Then he heard a concussive boom that made him think of a nuclear bomb dropping and he was going down into unconsciousness, left to contemplate what had just happened. There had been a certain stillness before he actually heard the boom. A quiet heaviness like he anticipated what was coming. Then it had hit, ripping through his insides, pulverizing his soul and exterminating thought.

He fought to stay conscious. Tried to think about the various pains all over his body. He told himself that if he succumbed to this, then he would never have an answer, would never find out about Elliot. But it was no use.

The rumbling had stopped.

The rain and the wind and the thunder and the lightning continued to howl on but they all seemed sedate in the aftermath of that boom.

He put his face down in the good fresh smell of the earth and slowly spiraled into the barbed black womb of unconsciousness.

Nine

Cassie made it into the woods before the hail hit. The dense, leafy canopy, despite the wind's attempt to peel it back, managed to keep the worst of the hail away. She wanted nothing more than to collapse somewhere and cry away the last fifteen minutes of her life but she kept running. She had to. Gregory was behind her. She didn't stop to see how far. The last time she had glanced over her shoulder he was coming up frightfully fast, one hand struggling to keep his pants up and the other pressed against a bloody eye socket.

The storm was the least of her worries.

In many ways the storm was her friend. It made it darker and the loud hammering of the rain punctuated by the thunder was very disorienting. *All the better to hide with*, she thought. Even though she was tempted to jaunt off to her left or right, she knew that would cause her to lose speed and ground. She continued straight forward, the trees scraping her face and arms as she ran past them.

She wondered at exactly what point her life had become a horror movie. There certainly wasn't a shred of reality to it anymore. This could not be happening to her.

It reminded her of the time she and two friends were caught

shoplifting some make-up at the mall. They were in one of the pricier boutiques, giggling and having fun, sliding this and that into their pockets. They had walked out of the store and into the mall, thinking they were safe, when a security guard told them to stop and follow him. That was the point when it became unreal. Everything else was just part of the dream. They had to empty their pockets and purses. Everything had to come out: the change, the keys, the Kleenex, the stolen lipsticks and eyeliners, the ample money they could have used to pay for those items, the birth control pills, the eighth of pot. All of these things were left on the security desk until each of their parents came to pick them up. The objects were pointed out to their parents as if to say, "See, look what bad children you have."

That was one of the reasons Cassie didn't get to take driver's education, why she didn't get her license last week when she turned sixteen, why Gregory had to escort her to and from school.

So maybe she could trace all of this back to that one incident.

But right now she had to concentrate on survival. Her heart pounded in her chest as she struggled against the rapid incline of the ground. The wind was vicious and she felt scoured by the rain, sticks, and dirt flying through the air. The first hill leveled off and she stopped to look behind her.

She couldn't see anything. The woods were dark anyway but now it might as well have been a moonless night. Lightning flashed and she searched frantically below her for any sign of Gregory. Just before the lightning faded she caught a brief glimpse, a darkened out-of-focus snapshot of him.

He stumbled up the hill less than six feet away from her.

And he saw her.

"Cassie!" his ragged voice cut through the rain.

She still held the book in her hand. She threw it at him, hoping to confuse him more than hit him. She took off again. She must have been on some kind of trail. The ground here was sandy and cleared. She took two steps to her right, hoping that would be the last thing Gregory saw before the lightning completely left, and then ran full speed to her left, her boots finding much better traction on the trail. This time her running was even more inspired. Gregory had looked pretty mangled. She figured he probably wanted to kill her on top of raping her, now.

As she ran she stuck a hand out and let it brush the wet trees as she passed. When her hand hit a branch of a decent size she squeezed it to see if it would come away easily. Finally she found one, gripped it tightly and held it in front of her like a bayonet.

Blindly, she ran on, ignoring the stitch in her side and the pain in her legs. Realizing Gregory was able to check and gauge her whereabouts every time the lightning struck she pushed on as hard as she could. She also realized that, as easy as the trail made running, it also gave Gregory wide-open visibility. Without breaking stride she darted to her right, bracing herself for the wet scrape of the shrubs and the slap of the tree leaves.

All at once, everything seemed to stop.

She stopped too.

She turned around.

Lightning flashed.

Gregory was less than ten feet behind her.

That's when she heard the boom. It took her breath and felt like it ripped the meat from her bones.

She saw an image of herself melting into the ground.

She screamed, her voice trailing away from her before she closed her eyes and dropped into the dense undergrowth.

Ten

While he was out, John had a dream.

Coming into the dream, a murky beginning, he stood in the backyard. It was winter. Snow came up well past the cuff of his jeans. He was without a jacket and the wind chilled his gooseflesh-twisted skin. His whole body felt tight. Setting a quick pace for himself, he started walking, crunching through the snow, headed back toward the expanse of woods that lay behind the winter-desolate crop field.

It seemed like the path had been chosen for him. On the surface of the snow, a purple line extended back to the woods. He couldn't tell if the line was actually there or if it was like the floaters that occasionally bounced across his eyes. In places, it looked like the line was physically melting through the snow. In other places, it looked like the line hovered above the snow.

A full moon hung overhead in the clear sky and the night was surprisingly bright, the skeletons of trees in the yard casting stark shadows on the crystalline snow. He had never liked winter. It had its moments of beauty, sure, but it also felt like a barren wasteland. No birds chirped, no animals skittered off in the distance. There weren't any signs of green life coming up all around him. It was just gray and white and black and more gray.

He hit the open field, grown up with corn all summer, now stripped bare, reaching back like a petrified ocean until it met the woods. The trees there, on the horizon, looked like bony fingers struggling to scrape blood from the sky just to give it some color. He drew his arms up around himself, lowered his head, and walked faster.

He covered the field in rapid dream-time. What would have probably taken him a good half an hour was covered in what felt like minutes.

As he drew nearer to the woods, his pulse quickened, warming him from the inside. The cold chills became an excited shiver up and down his spine, drawing his scrotum and anus tight. Struggling against the snow, he broke into a slow trot, keeping his eyes on that copse of woods. There the woods were like a finger, maybe only a quarter of a mile wide, reaching into the fields. He was always glad about that jutting extension of woods. Otherwise, all of his parents' land would be yard, crop field, and the one-time pasture that had become more of a meadow since they no longer kept any sheep or cattle.

From within the woods, he thought he saw more of that purplish light, pulsing like a heart. And there was something in the breeze floating toward him. It was the smell of summer and the spicy scent of night blooming flowers. He wanted to be wherever that scent was coming from. It quickened his step even further. In a few minutes he stood at the threshold of the woods looking for that purple womb in between the thick tree trunks.

The trees he could see were glistening, coated in ice. The wind blew and the branches clattered together, the thicker parts of the trees squeakily moaning.

He found the entrance to the foot worn trail and crossed into the woods.

The woods sloped downward toward a dry creek bed. A fire crackled down there. Breathing in the musky smoke, he went toward it.

The rest of the things, the rest of the *people*, he didn't see until he was right up on them.

The scene before him was so completely foreign it took him a few moments to orient himself.

The fire was larger than a campfire. It was at least as tall as him and, judging by the balmy climate around him, seemed totally unnecessary for anything other than a source of light.

His shivers intensified as he slowly took in the figures around the fire. He counted twelve. There was no telling them apart. They wore long black cloaks leaving only a flash of pale chin visible. Despite the warmth around him, his shivering grew harsher, his teeth clattering together. In front of the fire, on a makeshift waist-high wooden table, was a thirteenth. This one wore a robe also, but the hood was pulled down off her head. From John's vantage point, her face looked stunning. A sharp jaw line rose out of the cloak, capped by full lips. Her hair was black and shiny, extending down to the mound of her chest.

Was she a sacrifice? John wondered.

But this is just a dream, he reminded himself.

The people in the cloaks were chanting, low and rhythmic, matching with the pulse pounding in John's head.

The circle tightened around the woman on the table. *I guess it's an altar*, John thought.

The first figure raised its right arm, the fabric of the cloak tumbling back to reveal a pale white hand. The left hand grasped a large, thin knife, the tip of it hooked ever so slightly. John soon realized the rest of the figures grasped a similar device. Raising the dagger, the figure drew it across its right wrist and held it over the woman's mouth. John couldn't see the trickle of blood but he saw the drops landing on the woman's pale cheeks and chin. Her tongue snaked out and cleaned the area around her mouth.

The circle shifted clockwise and the next figure performed the same ritual.

If it wasn't a dream, if it didn't have all the qualities of a dream, John would have run far from all this. There was something inside of him telling him he was somehow involved. Something else told him he was all right. This was just a dream.

And everybody knew dreams couldn't hurt you.

And in the back of his head he was a seven-year-old again. A seven-year-old boy who has just been told his older brother is gone and he will probably never see him again. A small boy listening to the whispers in the hallway—

devils devils devils devils

clutching his pillow tightly and waiting for the world around him to collapse completely. He remembered the only things that kept him from sinking into total despair were his parents. He had to stay the way he was just for them.

"Would you like to talk to someone else about this?" his mother had asked him.

And he had said, *"No."*

He only wanted everything the way it had been and nothing could ever be like that again. There was only the void created by Elliot's disappearance and the vast mystery stretching out before him.

"What's a Devil?"

No answer.

Here, in front of him, the answer.

The answer? Was it?

Rapt, he watched as the circle slowly went around. The lower half of the woman's face became a glistening red and yet he found himself still wanting to kiss those lips. The thought both disgusted and aroused him. Beneath his shorts, he felt himself stiffening. This stiffening turned his stomach over, eating it up with acid. His heart continued to pound in his chest. The chanting had slowly risen in volume and sweat now trickled from his scalp and rolled down his face.

He had kept count in his head and was now eager to see what

would happen after the twelfth figure had drained itself into the woman. Eager for any kind of answer. Any kind of logic.

Dreams cannot solve mysteries.

The chanting was now loud enough for him to feel it in his bones.

The woman turned her head toward him and he found himself staring into her eyes, getting lost in them, trying to pull himself back out of them. They were dark, faintly blue-purple like the clear sky, like the pulsing womb he had sought. Maybe they were black and were only reflecting the sky. Her face was flawless, like burnished ivory. As much as he wanted to look away, as much as he wanted to be repulsed by her face, he couldn't, he wasn't.

He wanted the face and its owner and he wanted her to have nothing to do with Elliot's disappearance. John wanted them to be unrelated because there was something inside of him that was excited by what was happening around him. It was new. Something previously unfelt and it made him think of that crackling electrical storm feeling. Maybe he had always wanted some tornado to pick him up and carry him away to Oz, regardless of how dark and twisted that Oz was. As long as it was different and magical, maybe that was all that mattered.

He looked up at the bright white moon.

Only it wasn't full anymore.

The first thought he had was that it was being eaten by something.

It was slowly turning black until it was surrounded by nothing but a glowing ring of white.

As if to remind him of the possible treachery of this place, he felt hands touch him. Cold and thin, they were on his arms, his legs, and the back of his neck. Effortlessly, they lifted him and he didn't try and fight them off. They were carrying him toward *her.* Knowing otherwise, he told himself someone of her beauty wouldn't be able to perform evil.

Slowly, she slid off the altar, never unlocking her eyes from

John's.

She moved to the side and John took her place on the altar. She took her eyes away to study those around the altar as they shifted it so John stood upright, the warm wood at his back. While her eyes were diverted, John looked her up and down. The cloak didn't do a good enough job of hiding her scant curves. It only increased the mystery and desire raging through his head and body. Mystery, desire, and some indescribable fear. If it weren't for the area of his brain telling him he was dreaming he would have tried his hardest to get away. And he still wasn't sure if this was a dream or a nightmare. If he knew these people were the fabled Devils then, without question, he would not be here willingly.

Could he really be hurt in this dream place?

His arms were brought up over his head and fastened behind the altar.

The woman approached him, hypnotically slow, her eyes once again locking onto his. She reached out a hand, her fingernails tipped in black, and placed it against his cheek. Her touch felt soothing and cool. She slid her hand down his neck, the front of his shirt, stopping at the button on his jeans. She reached out her other hand and unfastened the buttons down the front of his jeans. Then she reached her hands into the waistband of his pants and underwear and tugged them down. The press of her hands against his hips canceled out the awkwardness he felt at being exposed in front of a group of people.

Remember, this is just a dream.

The woman moved her face close to his, their cheeks practically touching, and whispered, "Only the dead can leave."

And he forgot about everything else. He forgot about Elliot. He forgot about the mystery and, most of all, he forgot about trying to find any answers.

The woman eyed John's stiff member and dropped to her knees. She put her left hand under his scrotum and encircled the fingers of her right around the base of his cock. She rubbed her lips along the head, let her tongue flick out and run down its length. Then her mouth was around it, devouring the entire length, sucking on it. John had never felt this before. Even though it was a dream, he still felt all the warmth, all the forbidden intimacy of this woman pleasuring him in front of twelve others who chanted loudly and watched intently. He found himself enjoying the fact that they were being studied.

He tried not to let himself go. It felt too good to stop and he wondered if he should warn her. It seemed rude to just do that in someone's mouth.

It's just a dream.

The beginnings of his orgasm started at the base of his spine, incontestably stronger than anything he was able to produce with his hand. He felt his penis harden further, his scrotum tightening.

Then he felt the release he'd only felt at the clutch of his own hand.

He closed his eyes, trying to sense as much of it as he could.

The smoke from the fire smelled like incense.

The chanting rose in pitch.

His penis felt even more sensitive than it had before.

The woman's mouth pulled away.

He wanted to wake up and take a deep breath of relief.

The woman's lips moved to his thigh, closed over it.

Pain bloomed as her teeth punctured his skin.

His eyes shot open.

He wanted to wake up.

He looked at the woman, smiling up at him through a mask of blood and slowly receding into the darkness.

He wanted to wake up.

Another cloaked figure moved in front of him, dropped to its knees, pulled back its cloak. It was completely bald and pallid. Black eyes. John couldn't tell if it was male or female.

He wanted to wake up.

Eleven others took their turn in front of him. Indeterminate sex. Maybe even indeterminate species. They looked like monsters.

He wanted to wake up.

He thought about telling them he wasn't a water fountain.

He wanted to wake up.

The pain receded but he felt himself grow too weak to stand, the rope cutting into his wrists.

He wanted to wake up.

He looked up at the moon, now white and full again.

He wanted to wake up.

Eleven

Groggy, Gordon Fresk raised himself up to his feet. He knew the storm was supposed to be bad but he didn't know what the hell had happened before he lost consciousness. He was at the east end of the pasture, looking for John, when he had heard the boom. He didn't remember anything after that.

Now he stood in the pasture, confused and as scared as he had been since watching Gloria give birth to Elliot.

There was a heaviness in his bones that made him want to lie down. He checked his watch. Maybe the concrete measurement of time would help him orient himself.

Figures, he thought. The watch had stopped working. All the hands had fallen off.

Despite the nearly full moon, the night was incredibly dark. The thick ground fog didn't help matters much.

Feeling beaten, Gordon headed back toward the house, figuring John would be there by now. That's what brought him out into the goddamned pasture in the first place. He couldn't think of any possible reason as to why John wouldn't have come back inside. So, insisting Gloria head down to the cellar, Gordon had gone outside at the height of the storm to search for John. Maybe John had decided to wait the storm out in the barn. Anyway, he was certain to be back in the house by now.

Halfway back to the house Gordon realized something wasn't right. It was something with the view. He stopped, trying to figure it out. Something was missing.

It seemed like his heart stopped when he finally realized what it was.

The house wasn't there.

Beaten feeling or not, he took off running toward where the house used to be. As he drew closer he saw that the house wasn't *gone*—merely leveled.

Gloria! he thought. *John!*

He did an odd little dance standing there at the perimeter of the yard, turning in circles.

Maybe John hadn't made it back to the house. Maybe he was still out here somewhere. What about Gloria? Would the door on the cellar hold under the weight of the stone? Hell, would the *ceiling* of the cellar hold? It was concrete but still, he wondered. If the root from a tree could crack it…

He quickly threw together a game plan. Of course, the game plan hinged on John's not getting back into the house. He would go back into the pasture and yell for John. It would have to be easier for two people to pull the stones off the cellar than one. And, let's face it, Gloria was either trapped down there or dead under the weight of the heavy stones. He didn't want to think about the latter.

He ran back toward the pasture. "John!" he yelled. "John!"

The barn, he thought and veered off to his right, toward the driveway.

He saw the barn, black behind the milky fog. It looked like it had held up better than the house. Maybe the wood was more elastic or something. The roof was peeled back. Many boards had been stripped away, making him think of a maniacal, gap-toothed grin.

The barn had two levels. One was partially beneath the ground and formed the stone base of the barn. That was where the old stalls were. The second was where the hay and feed used to be kept. He assumed that, if anywhere, John was in the lower level.

He ran into the ground floor.

"John!" he called. "John! It's me! Can you hear me? Are you hurt?"

As impatient as he was, he stood there, waiting for John's response.

None came.

"Shit," he said.

He stormed back out of the barn and into the night air.

He ran back toward the middle of the pasture, toward the pond, scanning all around him for any signs of movement.

Then he saw something. Didn't he? Was that a person off to his right? Did it just move or was it one of the fledgling cedars?

"John?" he said.

Black behind the fog, the figure shifted. It had to be John, didn't it? But why wasn't he saying anything?

He jogged toward the figure until he got close enough to make out the features.

"John," he said, relieved.

Then he regretted letting his guard down. The thing in front of him was only partially John. The face was John's but the mouth seemed too full of teeth. And it was taller than John. Its arms hung down to its knees, the fingers long and curving into thick, savage-looking claws. It looked like what John would look like if he had been designed to kill. Something inside Gordon screamed at him that this wasn't his boy. Couldn't possibly be.

He turned, not knowing if he was going toward the house or not. He just wanted away from the thing behind him. Adrenaline and fear were the only things that moved his legs. He quickly wished he hadn't run all the way over here.

He heard John (*not John*, his mind screamed at him) behind him.

Felt John's (*not John's*) breath on the back of his neck.

John reached a hand around Gordon's face, one of his claws puncturing his right eye before hitting the back of his skull.

Gordon screamed and gurgled. John yanked him to the ground. Then he dragged him by his eye socket over to the pond.

There, using his claws, he laid his father's skin open. He reached in, felt the vital organs as the vitality slowly left them. Various pools of blood bloomed all over Gordon's body as John moved his hands over the skin. John stuck his head into one of the pools and let his long tongue snake down into it, tasting the blood, drinking the blood and getting full from it.

His first kill was a large one and the hunt was over for the night. John ran around the pasture feeling the moisture on his skin, tasting the fog mingling with the blood on his tongue.

Eventually, he found his way back to his kill, his father, and curling up next to the dwindling warmth, he fell asleep.

Twelve

The first thing Cassie felt when she woke up was the heat enshrouding her like a nuclear blanket. She wondered where the hell she was. What memories she had seemed grim and far away. She tried to grasp a single shred of those memories, anything that would give her some clue as to where she was and how she got here when she felt something smack into her lower back. The sun was so intense she had to have been here overnight.

She bent in pain, her bare arm and side scraping along the ground.

She remembered Gregory and some of the other stuff but it was still unclear. She tried to scramble to her feet and realized her feet and hands were bound.

She squinted up and saw Gregory wielding a stick, the sun burning above his head.

"You're not getting away this time," he said. "I've seen to that."

He was a frightening sight towering above her. His right eye was a dark red mass, dried blood caking his cheek. She hoped the eye was gone but it was swollen too badly for her to tell. He had taken off his shirt, his almost womanly breasts and large gut disgusting her. She noticed her shirt was also gone and didn't take the time to think the shirts were probably what bound her. She continuously wriggled her hands and feet, trying to break out of her ties.

"You don't want to do this, Gregory," she said.

"Tell me why not."

He reached the stick down between her legs and raised her skirt with it.

"It's rape, for one thing. It hurts."

"It won't hurt me. Besides, you've already done that. I think you put out my eye. The way I see it, you deserve it."

"I was trying to defend myself."

"Didn't have to put my eye out."

Something snapped in Cassie. Something told her she wasn't going to be able to talk him out of what he was going to do. She quickly told herself two things. One, she wasn't going to make it easy for him. Two, she wasn't going to let him see her cry.

She looked up at him and tried to make eye contact but the sun was too invasive.

"If you just want some pussy you could get a fucking whore!" she shouted at him.

"A whore costs money."

"You don't go to jail for fucking a whore."

"Maybe I'll have to kill you when I'm finished. Besides, you're a whore anyway. Who else lets boys fuck them when they're fifteen? Look at you, wearing a black bra and panties and trying to convince me you're not a whore."

"Rape!" Cassie screamed. "Help me! Somebody, please, help me!"

"Shut up," Gregory said, reaching out and cracking her over the head with the stick.

She lurched toward him, gnashing her teeth, trying to bite his leg. He cracked her with the stick again, smacking her back to the ground.

"You're probably right," she spit at him. "A *whore* wouldn't even want to fuck you, no matter how much you paid her. Look at yourself. You're a fucking monster. You're *ugly*. You're *stupid*. You have *boobs*, for Christ's sake. I hope you do kill me after you rape me because I don't want to have to live another second after you've been inside me."

"Shut up." He smacked her with the stick again, knocking her back onto the ground, a rock digging into her shoulder. "Bitch."

He fumbled with her skirt and she shifted back and away from him, pressing harder against the rock. He was sweating, breathing heavily, his big clumsy hands shaking as he tugged at the skirt. Painful seconds passed and he stopped trying to work the tricky clasp at the side of the skirt. He rose to his knees and unfastened the button and zipper of his pants.

While he was looking down, trying to focus on his stained pants with one eye, she brought her bound forearms down below her head and grabbed the rock between her small hands, hoping it wasn't lodged in the dirt. Here was another reason to celebrate Gregory's stupidity, she thought. He had bound her legs and, in order to properly rape her, would have to remove himself from the straddling position he currently inhabited. Realizing this, he stood up and shucked down his pants and underwear, his sex fully aroused.

She had to do it now. Once he got his weight back on her, she was gone.

She grabbed the rock as tightly as she possibly could. She waited for him to lift his left leg out of his pants, putting all of his weight on the right.

All the anger about Gregory and this whole situation surged through her. She lurched forward, swinging the heavy rock in her bound arms, letting it create its own momentum.

There was a smack and a pop.

Gregory screamed and Cassie listened as the scream tapered away into a growl.

Everything went into some form of slow motion. There was a moment where he seemed to waver before, unable to support his weight, the wrecked knee buckled and he fell to his right.

Struggling, she managed to get to her feet.

She wasn't sure what she wanted to do. Part of her wanted to totally demolish Gregory. She didn't want to have to worry about him anymore, his threatening presence. He had already firmly established the fact he could not be trusted. Another part of her told her she shouldn't do that. As long as he was injured and harmless, it would be wrong to finish him off.

She watched as he writhed around on the floor of the woods, clutching his bloodied knee, naked and defenseless.

With everything that had happened she was somewhat amazed she was able to stand so well and feel so strong.

"I could kill you right now," she said. "Do you know that?"

"Fuck you."

Not fully knowing why, she bent and smashed the rock into his left leg, above the kneecap. When not out for survival, the instinct to cripple was not really there. That was just to inflict pain.

"Want me to do that again?"

This time he bared his teeth and snarled at her.

"What happened to you?"

"Leave me alone," he barked.

"Fine." She turned and hopped back toward the woods.

It was then, trying to find some direction to walk, that she realized how confused and disoriented she actually was. She really didn't have any idea where she was. She had no idea what time it was although she was pretty sure it was morning. She felt totally filthy and beaten and miserable. She didn't know what had turned Gregory into such a beast. And should she even think of the sonic earth rumbling boom that had taken her to her knees in the first place? Things had been going well for her the past several months. Now it seemed everything had fallen apart all at once. Perhaps, if she had more energy, if it wasn't so fucking *hot*, then she wouldn't feel so overwhelmed. Instead, because it felt like her mind and body were too exhausted to do anything else, she formed a very simple idea of what she would do. She would only do what she could. She had to remove the binding from her arms and legs. It was just fabric, after all. She assumed Gregory had intended it as more of a hindrance, something to slow her down until he could smother her in his girth, more than an actual shackling device. She couldn't imagine they would be very hard to remove.

Why was it so incredibly hot?

That was strange for this early in the morning. She felt like it had to be morning. The thought of being unconscious all night was only as unfathomable as everything else that had been happening to her.

It didn't feel like there was any moisture to the air at all.

Maybe, after she removed the shirts, she would go in search of water. She hoped she was on the reserve somewhere because, after last night and this morning, she felt like she really needed something to drink. She knew a river ran through the reserve.

And after she found that, she supposed she would find a place where she could see Gregory but he couldn't see her and wait for something to happen.

It amazed her she wasn't scared yet. It must be the fatigue, she told herself. Why wasn't she struggling to rip the bindings off and running back to where she had come from? After all, there were a lot of things to be afraid of. Like Gregory. Like the storm of near-supernatural proportions. Like the threat of heat exhaustion. Like the boom. *What was that boom?* She wondered if her family was okay. She wondered how this would all end. *It would be as simple as walking home, wouldn't it?* She wondered why all the leaves on all the trees were dead and why she hadn't noticed that the world around her, the world that should have been green, was now brown. And she wondered why getting home probably wouldn't be as simple as walking there because even though she had a pretty good idea of where she was she still felt some place entirely different, as though she were standing at the edge of some horrifically fantastic adventure, the ending of which might be a long way away.

She found a tree with very rough bark and began scraping the cloth binding her hands against it.

This, she thought. This is all I will think about.

Thirteen

By the time John woke up, the day had become an oven, stifling
and oppressive. It pressed down around him, making it difficult to
paw through his freshly awakened mind and seize upon any single
thought. The first thing he remembered was his dream. He tried to
categorize it—dream or nightmare—and couldn't do it. His brain
felt choked. He couldn't seem to remember the dream in any kind
of linear pattern. He remembered the woman, a thing of beauty,
and the place, another thing of beauty—a slice of summer evening
in the winter. Of course, it was summer now, but there didn't seem
to be anything pleasant in this summer. There was something else
in his head too, some other aspect of the dream, but he couldn't
figure out what it was. It was something like a gap in his memory.
Maybe it had something to do with Elliot. He just couldn't grasp it.
The only thing he could grasp was a sinking feeling of doom and
despair he would rather forget.

He lay in the grass, the heat clinging to his skin, slicking it with
sweat. And even though he couldn't be completely sure about the
nature of last night's dream he felt relieved to be awake.

There are no answers in dreams.

But he wasn't so sure of that. If the answers weren't in dreams then maybe they *were* in that warped dream world and he wasn't so sure the answers would be the ones he wanted to hear.

He guessed the seriousness of last night's storm had passed and he stood up, ready to resume normalcy, ready to dismiss the past twelve hours as a fucked up event he could file away in his memory bank.

But when he stood up, nothing was right. Nothing was normal.

Dead things surrounded him.

He was over by the pond, which was about where he thought he was when he lost consciousness.

To his left lay his father. John went over to him and crouched down on his knees. Shock stripped away his emotions. His father was mutilated. One of his eyes was a blackened, bloody hole. His clothes were shredded into wet crimson tatters. Gouges split his skin beneath where the clothes were sliced open. In a thudding heartbeat, the nightmare was immediately upon him, twitching and scurrying beneath his skin.

He placed a hand on his father's cheek and leaned his head down until it rested on the man's chest. He stayed that way for some time, sobbing, knowing no amount of tears would bring his father back. The absence, the new void created by this atrocity was the only thing he could think about. It wasn't entirely a new void. He had felt this void before, had been feeling it for the past twelve years. This was merely an addition to the void, an intensification. He didn't think about who could have done this or why. He didn't think about the complete bizarreness of the situation. He simply didn't think. He mourned and sobbed. Having gone through this before and having a little more maturity now, it was like he knew how to completely shift his emotions so the whole crazy world didn't spiral even further out of control.

Dazed, he stood back up and wiped his tears and sweat-soaked hair from his forehead.

His father wasn't the only thing that was dead.

Bloated fish and frogs lined the pond. The most noticeable were the albino catfish his father had stocked the pond with last year. Some of them were the length of John's forearm, twice the diameter.

There must have been a hundred of them. He had always found catfish to be sort of strange and now there seemed to be something completely alien about them. Dead and lifeless, eyes glazed over, staring up at the harsh blue sky. Not covered in scales like the other fish but slick and hairless with those long rubbery whiskers reaching away from their mouths, trailing out into the grass. Those whiskers would be the first things to rot, he thought.

The grass, green as of yesterday, was now brown and dry and brittle-looking—winter grass or draught grass. The cedars and spruce trees dotting the meadow were a rust-brown color. He remembered how his biology teacher had told them evergreens were a good site indicator for pollution, urging them to look at the deadened trees along the state route and wonder exactly what it was they breathed in every day.

To say something was definitely wrong would have been the understatement of the century.

He looked toward the house and saw the devastation there. It did not, at this point, surprise him to see the house lying in a broken heap. He wondered about his mom and wondered if he needed to worry about her. It stood to reason she would be dead, too.

This cannot be happening.

All the horrors that had happened twelve years ago had, overnight, gathered themselves together and launched a full-scale attack on him. Part of him wanted to go back to that strange dream world—

the Devils

Something else to think about. Something else to fear. Some childish nightmare spooks slowly proving they *did* have teeth and they *could* bite and they had the ability to crawl outside of his head and wreak havoc on the world around him.

All of these things swirled through his head and he found himself oddly calm.

This was not anything that hadn't happened before.

The Devils

would reveal themselves and then he would have them. He would know about them and he would tell others.

But he would have to wait. He couldn't go chasing them but, dream or not, he felt he was involved with them. The disappearance of his brother and the death of his father aside, he felt like the Devils, whoever they were, were now a part of him.

For now, there was no time for insane thoughts. There were things that needed to be done.

He didn't know where to begin.

Off in the distance, a good half-mile beyond his house, he saw that the neighbors' house was still intact.

Going there seemed to be the best bet. He could call the police, tell them about his dad, tell them his mother was missing. But he couldn't tell them about the Devils because because because…

The Devils don't exist.

Yes they do, he told himself. Maybe logic had to be shut down. He was dealing with dreams and mysteries now.

And he thought back to the Hixon book he'd just read. He didn't know who the guy was. John had only ordered the book on Amazon because he liked the cover and the title and it was set in a town called Lynchville. The author's bio said he lived in Illinois and the book never said what state the fictitious Lynchville was in. John hadn't even thought of the Devils until yesterday during the storm. The more he thought about it now, the more he was convinced the author knew. John wished the book wasn't buried in the house.

He felt himself getting sidetracked again.

As if to reassert that his rational mind was a faulty engine and bring himself to the problem at hand he wondered why there wasn't somebody at the farm already. It seemed odd. He remembered the loud boom from the previous night and figured there had to be others who had heard it as well. Surely one of the neighbors had seen the collapsed house and assumed there was a group of highly distressed people inside it. And why wasn't one of the park rangers out here? He knew they would have called his dad into work last night, to help clear away any trees that had been blown down, and he was sure there had been. The ranger station was less than a mile down the road. It seemed like one of them would have driven by out of suspicion and seen the obvious damage that had occurred to this area.

The fact that none of this had happened made him wonder if this wasn't maybe a more universal thing.

Maybe everybody was busy with their own disasters. Or maybe there wasn't anybody left.

Maybe the madness had crept away from the Fresk family to infect everyone else.

This gave him all the more reason to walk to the neighbors' house.

It would give him time to think, maybe come up with some type of plan.

As much as he wanted to crawl into some nice cool place and collapse—to grieve, to mourn, to cry, to question everything around him—he knew that wasn't an option.

He walked toward the driveway, noticing as he went that the cornfield separating the meadow from the driveway had also gone brown and brittle-looking like at harvest time, except the stalks didn't even reach his knee.

His bones felt leaden but he didn't rush. He figured the disaster had already happened and there wasn't anything he could do about it. The best thing he could do right now was to keep a level head. Judging by the position of the sun in the sky, he reasoned that it was a little after noon. For some reason, maybe it was the heat, he found himself longing for night.

Fourteen

It took him at least twenty minutes to get even halfway there. The air around him didn't feel right. It wasn't humidity. On humid days, John knew the air would look kind of hazy. The sky overhead wouldn't be so crystalline blue. Nevertheless, there was some kind of palpability to the air. Starting out, he had the thought of having to cut his way through the air to get where he was going, like traveling through a thick jungle or increased gravity. And it only seemed to get harder the farther he went.

Fields lined each side of the driveway. The driveway ran east to west. He was a quarter of the way through the north field, on the far side of the driveway, when he felt like he couldn't go on anymore. All the muscles in his body were drawn up. All of this tension throughout his body snaked into his head, filling it, making it heavy. The feeling reminded him of extreme fatigue. He imagined his head filled with dense clouds. The blooming heaviness threatened to pull him to the ground.

He tried to press forward and couldn't do it. He gathered up all the strength he had and tried to throw his torso forward. A heavy, near-electrical shock surged its way through his body, cutting through the marrow of his bones. He quickly pulled back and the shock slowly dissipated. Again gathering up everything he had, he tried to pass forward. And the strange electrical surge greeted him almost like there was some kind of imaginary line in the field that could not be crossed.

"Fuck," he said and took an even bigger, more forceful, step forward.

Another sudden surge of that metal heaviness shot through his body, this time driving him down on one knee. He felt something trickling out of his nose and dismissed it as sweat until it splotched onto his bare knee, a blooming rose of blood. He pressed his head against his upper arm and wiped it on his shirt. He told himself not to panic. He was not going to bleed to death. His bloody nose probably wasn't even related to this. He got them all the time. "Your nose was just dry," his mother would say.

With great effort he stood up and took a few steps to his left, walking along that imaginary line as though it were some kind of prison fence, before turning and heading in the direction he had originally intended.

Again, the dull, heavy shock and he reeled, collapsing back into the crinkly corn. The previous shocks had taken it out of him. This one was almost too much.

Standing up and looking around, he cursed himself. He hadn't been paying attention. The line wasn't an imaginary one. It was very real. Over here, on his side, the corn was dead and brown but, immediately in front of him, it was green and maybe even a fraction taller.

Does corn grow that fast? he wondered. He guessed it probably did.

Now, turning in a slow circle, he squinted into the afternoon brightness, scanning for more signs of the boundary. To the north, it ended right in front of him. To the west, it ended just before the road—which ruled that out. To the south, he thought he could see where it ended at the far side of the meadow. The trees at the fence line wavered lush and green in a breeze that didn't exist where he stood. To the east, toward the woods, he couldn't see any sign of the dead area ending.

That would have to be an option, he told himself. If he couldn't leave this area, then it stood to reason he would have to find someone in this area who could help him. There were people to the north and south, but that line was there and he now knew there wasn't any crossing the line. But maybe, he thought, it wouldn't be the same for people coming from the *other* side of the line. Maybe, if he went down to the road, someone driving by would see him. Surely there had to be some way out of this. He had a hard time grasping the ridiculousness of the situation. The fact there was some prescribed area he couldn't escape from almost made him want to laugh. And it wasn't like a fence or anything. He could probably get past it if he could deal with the physical sensation it caused him. Maybe another person would have a different reaction.

Slowly, he backed away from the line since that was where the air seemed to be at its heaviest and most draining. He immediately felt a little better. He walked toward the gravel driveway, wiping his bloody nose off on the back of his hand. The blood flow had decreased even this far from the line. Once reaching the driveway he hitched his shorts up on his hips and turned to walk toward the road.

Fifteen

After what felt like hours, Cassie finally ripped the fabric binding her hands. It was stupid, she knew, but she felt an amazing sense of freedom wash over her. Quickly, she bent down and untied the big knot of the shirt that had been wrapped around her ankles. Despite the new found freedom she had, she was still exhausted, her hands shaking as she flapped the fabric out in front of her. This must have been Gregory's, she thought. It was huge. This meant hers was the shredded heap behind her. She found the idea of wearing Gregory's shirt completely repulsive but she found the thought of him ever seeing her any way other than fully-clothed even more repulsive.

She didn't even want to think about him anymore.

But she had to.

She had to recognize him as being dangerous. That had probably been her mistake before. His actions from earlier had completely surprised her but, on some deeper level, she wasn't really surprised at all.

Creeping back through the woods, she found an area where she could see him, lying there on the ground, but he couldn't see her. She didn't want him to know she was there. She knew that, if he was aware of her presence, he would ask for some kind of help or try and talk to her like he hadn't done anything wrong. She didn't want to hear that. She didn't want to hear him.

Standing there, buttoning up her oversized shirt, she watched him. His right knee was huge and swollen and purple. He pulled up his filthy khaki pants and his underwear, supporting himself with his crooked left knee to heave his heavy buttocks off the ground. Some part of Cassie enjoyed this, watching him struggle with a task that should have been so very simple. She thought her ride home from school should have been simple too.

Another part of her felt bad. She knew he was just a sad, ugly, fat unpopular kid and if they didn't come from his parents, he wasn't going to get any breaks in life. And, in a way, she felt a little bit guilty about doing the things she had done to him. She wished she didn't have to feel this range of emotions. Because, she knew, not only was she watching him to make sure he couldn't get up and come after her, she was also watching him to make sure he was okay.

Quietly, she stood and watched as he grunted and rolled himself over, trying to drag himself along on his arms, screaming as his swollen knee scraped along the bumpy ground.

She knew what she had to do. The best thing she could do would be to get out of these woods and find some other person and find out what the fuck had happened. Then she could tell them about Gregory and someone could be sent to help him.

First she needed her boots. She had had all the discomfort she could stand. She didn't want the added pleasure of trudging through the floor of the woods barefoot on top of that.

She walked out to the narrow clearing where Gregory struggled along.

"Gregory."

He stopped his pull-and-drag and slumped his head. "What?"

"What did you do with my boots?"

He didn't say anything.

She moved closer to him, careful to remain out of arm's reach, thinking maybe he hadn't heard her.

"Gregory," she said slowly and loudly. "What did you do with my boots?"

He didn't answer her with words. He lunged at her, knocking her backwards and smothering her lower half with his weight. She cursed herself for not keeping the rock or a stick or anything. But there wasn't any time for that. His huge hands were on her shoulders and he was pulling himself up on her, any hopes for getting away decreasing as more of his weight was placed upon her.

She tried to scoot backwards but she was flattened between the ground and Gregory.

Now she felt like he had totally forgotten about raping her. Now she was pretty sure he just wanted her dead. He wrapped his huge hands around her thin neck.

Whatever lingering sympathies she had for him were now gone entirely.

Jesus, she was so fucking tired of fighting. Maybe she should just let him finish her off and then she could just lie dead in the dirt, food for wild animals and worms. What else could she do? She was smashed, exhausted, unable to breathe.

She searched his eyes, trying to find some scrap of sanity or humanity to appeal to.

Nothing.

Just the one eye gone mad and burning with a hateful vacancy.

And the other eye a bloody swollen mound of flesh.

It felt like the oxygen was leaving her muscles. Her hands clenched and unclenched, scraping along the ground and the dead leaves and the dirt.

All the debris. All the debris. Just beneath her hand, scraping along her palm.

She fisted the dirt and the dead leaves, feeling their good grittiness in her hands. Bringing both hands in front of Gregory's face, she ground the debris into his eye sockets. She knew this couldn't really give him any more pain than he was already in, but the initial sting, the initial burn, she knew, would surprise him. And she took this split second of surprise to free her neck from the hands of the beast and quickly scoot away while again smashing her hands into his eye sockets.

Suddenly she was out from beneath him and standing up and dashing away and... there they were.

Her boots.

Both of them situated neatly at the base of a huge tree.

Vampires in Devil Town, more damaged and significantly water bloated, lay next to them.

She sat down and pulled her boots on. She was maybe eight feet beside Gregory.

Even though she knew it probably wasn't the truth, she said, "I'm leaving you out here to rot, Greggie." She picked up the book and threw it at him. The water had added weight and it made a satisfying sound when it hit his head. "Here's something to read while you're dying, fucker."

He groaned, rolling around on his back.

"You won't be able to go anywhere," he grunted.

"Fuck you. You can't touch me now, you piece of shit."

"Everything's changed."

"You're fucking nuts, fat boy."

"The boom. It changed everything."

"You're finished scaring me, *Greggie*. I'm leaving you here to die."

"Go ahead. You'll see. Bitch."

Wanting to get away as fast as she could, she ran away from Gregory, into the woods.

Sixteen

Maybe the boom had affected him or made him sick in some way. It felt like something was inside of John. Maybe it was the lingering effect of being shocked by the strange perimeter.

The walk to the end of the driveway, less than a quarter of a mile, had exhausted him.

And still that feeling of heaviness, made even worse by his sweat-drenched clothes hanging from his body.

The exhaustion was both mental and physical. The slightest movement seemed to take an extreme amount of energy. Thoughts swirled around in his head, everything hitting him all at once.

You're losing sight of what you need to do, he thought. *You're down here waiting for help. Waiting for a car to pass. Do not think about anything else.*

He was so tired. He didn't even know how much longer he could stand up.

And just where was this magic line anyway? He could see that the corn on the other side of the road was still green but just where was the line drawn? Was it on his side of the road, on the other side, or somewhere in the middle?

Suddenly, this seemed of absolutely vital importance.

If the line was on the far side of the road, then this car watching bit was probably a fruitless exercise. That would mean the east to west lines blocked the road also. Assuming that if someone trying to get into the dead area had as hard a time getting in as he had getting out, then there wasn't a car that could get to him.

If the line was somewhere in the middle, then his chances were 50/50. Maybe he would see a car and maybe he wouldn't.

The best-case scenario, of course, would be that the line was on his side of the road. That way, at least a car *could* pass him on the road and might be able to at least see him there.

He wished he had the materials necessary to make a "HELP" sign or something. He guessed he would have to settle for frantically waving his arms and shouting. The road they lived on, Spring Road, was not heavily traveled. He had absolutely no idea how long he would have to wait before someone actually passed. Now was the time to find out if anybody *could* pass. He didn't know if he could stand the feel of the shock again but he knew he had to. At least now he knew what to expect.

His entire body tense, he stepped forward, preparing for either the shock or the transition from the gravel of his driveway to the somewhat smoother asphalt.

He got the shock. It ripped through his body, sizzling his insides, punching through his head. He felt the blood run out of his nose as he sank down onto the hot gravel. Lying there he told himself that, on the bright side, he probably wouldn't have to feel the shock again anytime soon.

Now he just had to wait.

He brought himself to his feet and stumbled over to the north side of the driveway. His mother had landscaped this area by placing a huge flat rock (perfect for sitting) beneath a huge ash tree. Since there hadn't been any wind or rain since the boom, the brown leaves were still on the tree and it offered a little bit of shade from the harsh sun.

He sat down on the rock and cleared his mind.

He didn't know how long he sat there. Even time didn't seem

right anymore. This time of year, it didn't get really dark until about nine or nine-thirty and yet sunset wasn't that far off. Even though he knew he couldn't have been awake more than a few hours, the sun was already low in the western sky which meant it was late afternoon or early evening.

Don't think about it.

Nothing makes sense anymore.

Only the dead can leave.

What did that *mean, anyway?*

Don't think about it. Don't think about it. Don't think...

Just sit and wait for a car to come.

Wait.

Wait.

Wait.

What happened in the next few minutes would reassure him in his current thought that nothing was logical and nothing made sense.

In the glowing purple twilight, he saw a car coming toward him from the south. No, it was a truck. Its headlights were on and it was coming fast down the road just when John had started to think maybe the whole world was dead or crazy. But he couldn't *hear* the truck, only see it.

He stood up and hobbled to the end of the driveway, careful not to take the slightest step toward the road because he couldn't possibly take the shock again. In anticipation of the truck's passing, he jumped up and down and flapped his arms wildly, trying to get the driver's attention.

But things fell apart and hope drifted away.

The truck did slow down and he heard it only it no longer sounded anything at all like a truck. It sounded like a train he was standing too close to, squealing and rumbling through his head. The truck slowed to a stop and John stood there, breathlessly staring at it. He didn't see the outside of the truck. It was like some strange X-ray where he saw the workings and mechanisms driving the truck, the pumping engine, and the driver sitting inside. The driver was not the flesh and meat of a vital human but a rotten, decayed skeleton. The driver turned its head toward John and everything melted away. Not just melted but *powered* into the ground—down and down and then gone completely.

The feeling John got when he tore his eyes away from this was an even stranger one. Like being in two worlds at the same time because when he backed away and looked north down the road he saw the truck from behind, sun glinting off it as it traveled away into whatever reality John had fallen out of.

He didn't really know what he wanted to do. He just knew he wanted to be away from the road so he turned and ran toward the woods, way off behind the ruins of his house. In the sweet purple of the early night, he bounded along like a boy chasing dreams.

Seventeen

Luckily, the storm hadn't ended up being that bad. There weren't any tornados. A tree had been struck by lightning over on Creek Road and Dan had had to go help with that. Someone had hit a deer down the road from the station but that happened on a monthly basis. That night, he had ended up making it home relatively on time and now he was back at the station with no worries.

At least, he continued telling himself there wasn't anything to worry about, but he couldn't stop thinking about the strange stuff he had seen on the night of the storm.

He hadn't told anyone else about it. Not even his wife, Arlene.

Some things, he figured, were just rare sights of beauty. Something to be remembered and nothing else. He wanted to convince himself nothing had come from what he had seen. That they were both simply spectacles and not really signs of anything of greater importance.

But there was still this lingering sensation.

Animals did not just run out of the forest. Especially during a massive thunderstorm. Those woods were their home. They *used* the woods for shelter and protection.

And, despite scouring the paper today and staying tuned to the police scanner, he still hadn't found a way to sufficiently explain away the flash he saw and the boom he heard. And that glow coming from around Gordon's house. There was a part of Dan that wanted to call Gordon, make sure he was doing okay. Another part of him told him just to leave Gordon alone and let him enjoy his vacation.

Dan really wanted to do that. He was sure that would be the best thing to do. He was fifteen years Gordon's senior and ever since Elliot had gone missing, Dan had felt like he had assumed the role of older brother. Dan had a protective streak, having two actual younger brothers, and he recognized that look of raw hurt that blossomed in Gordon's eyes every now and then.

But, dammit, the nagging feeling wouldn't leave him alone. He guessed it wouldn't be too bad if he drove by the Fresks' house. He didn't have to stop or anything. He could just drive by, a little slower than usual and make sure everything was in one piece. If their cars were there and nothing had burnt down or blown up, he would just make himself assume they were okay and keep right on driving. And if they had left town for vacation and one of the cars was missing, then maybe he would drive up to the house and poke around a little bit. Explore. Just so that feeling would go away.

Dan had a lot of "feelings," something that would start as a rumble in his belly or a tickle in his throat before becoming something resembling full-fledged nausea. Those feelings were seldom wrong.

Grabbing the keys from the little hook drilled in next to the door, he stepped out into the oppressive heat.

This was about the time when he went on his patrol of the reserve anyway. So what if he backtracked a little?

He hopped into the cab of the truck and cranked up the air conditioning. He made a left out of the station parking lot, traveling north. Gordon lived less than a mile from the station, on the right hand side.

Dan felt the nausea slowly creep up the back of his throat. He didn't know what he expected to find, exactly.

His first wave of ease washed over him as he drove up on a hill and saw Gordon's house standing placidly on its little knoll. Another few seconds and he was at their driveway feeling guilty, feeling like he was somehow spying on them. The only reason Dan felt like that was because Gordon had mentioned it one time. He wasn't being harsh or argumentative. It had been when they were working to dislodge a tree from the dam after a flood. Dan had wanted to do all the dangerous work and he said something about John not being able to lose Gordon too and Gordon had stopped what he was doing and told Dan he could take care of himself and didn't need Dan to do it for him. Then Gordon insisted on performing the most dangerous parts and, despite the fact he had never done them before, performed them with expert agility, saving Dan an amazing amount of physical effort.

That had been a long time ago but, whatever Gordon had said, Dan understood. Gordon didn't want to feel like anyone was watching out for him because that made him feel like a kid. They were both adults and Dan was, by nature, a helpful, protective person. And maybe that was why he liked working with Gordon so much. It made Dan self-aware. Maybe a little self-critical too but, hell, he figured that was probably normal for a man his age.

The crazy jitters he had been feeling since the storm went away. There stood Gordon's house, Gordon's barn. The family's three cars were all parked haphazardly around the driveway. It was a beautiful, almost nature parkish sprawl. Dan got the impression everything was okay with the Fresk homestead.

He got that impression but he still *felt* differently. He still felt like something had happened there or maybe it was just going to happen. But his feelings had been wrong before. They were not fool-proof by any means. Trying to find out if his feelings were right or not was not worth risking a rift in a great friendship.

Dan was just going to let it go. He was sure Gordon would show up at work the next week and everything would be fine. Everything would be just fine.

Eighteen

Cassie had never been good with directions. Maybe that was part of the problem. Initially, she had started running through the woods before realizing, with all the ups and downs, all the obstructions, it would be impossible to continue at that pace. Something about the air seemed thick anyway. She didn't really think it felt the same as humidity. Just *thick*.

This sense of heaviness, along with the heat, the hunger, the lack of sleep, and the bruised and battered body, made her feel like she had been wandering for hours. That's when she gave up. Just for the time being, she told herself. Despite the wandering, she couldn't see any signs of the woods ending. She didn't even know how far she and Gregory had made it into the woods to begin with.

Mental and physical exhaustion combined within her, begging her to find a nice soft comfortable spot in the late afternoon glow and lie down.

Part of her mind told her she needed to push on. Another part told her it didn't matter. She had no idea how to get out of the woods and she figured, at this point, *someone* had to be out looking for her. She was sure they could find her much easier than she could find them.

And there was the Gregory Factor. She didn't want to be around if he ever happened to get moving again. But she really didn't think that was going to happen unless Gregory's will was a lot stronger than she thought it was. Even if he was able to become mobile, what were the chances he would find her? Slim, at best, she guessed.

For right now, she didn't need to worry about anything. She just needed rest and sleep. She needed to replenish her muscles and void her brain of all the thinking that had ricocheted around it the past twenty-four hours or so.

She found a spot beneath two grown together honeysuckle bushes, dead leaves still adorning them, making it almost dark. The ground was cool and moist. The dirt smelled clean. Things almost felt right. Cassie drifted off.

She woke up wishing she had slept forever. Dusk had come over the woods. For the first time, it actually hit her that these weren't the same woods she had entered during the storm. The trees in these woods were brown and crunchy-looking, the trees of late fall, not early summer. But that was just something to wonder and speculate about. Something else to drive her insane.

Her entire body ached. She could no longer discern one wound from the other. The short nap did nothing to relieve the aching heavy feeling in her body. Maybe that was just from all the running and physical stuff she didn't normally do. And then there were the various cuts and bruises she attributed to Gregory.

Just thinking of him startled her. Sliding out of the little honeysuckle bush hut, she looked around for any sign of him. She didn't like that feeling at all. If there was one reason for her to hate him, that was it—the security he had completely stripped away from her.

Her ears rang as though she had awoken from a loud dream. Even though she did not want to hear Gregory, she wanted to hear *somebody*. Somebody who would come and lead her out of the woods that had gone dark and dead and show her back to her house on Maple Street.

But the woods were abnormally quiet. When her and some friends had camped in this area, she remembered thinking, with all the noises, it was actually louder than her house in town. So much for the quiet countryside. But now, as night drew over the woods, there wasn't a sound except for the occasional dry leaf falling to the ground. It was merely something odd, she thought, not wasting too much of her imagination. *That* was being spent on too many other things.

She stood up and looked around the dark, quiet woods. Maybe it was an irrational fear, but she was terrified to move. She couldn't explain it. She just kept thinking that if she tried to find her way out, she would either run into Gregory or wander deeper into the woods, farther away from anyone who might be searching for her.

Listen, she told herself. *There isn't anyone searching for you. This is quiet quiet. You would be able to hear if someone took so much as a footstep.*

This is all Gregory's fault.

Standing there, rooted, planted like one of the dead trees around her, she thought about what she would do to Gregory if she did meet up with him and was capable of overpowering him.

First thing, she wanted to remove his testicles. She didn't care how. Preferably, the most messily brutal way possible. She imagined her ragged fingernails digging into his thin, sensitive skin and simply ripping his scrotum away from his body. Then she wanted to shove his balls down his fucking throat. She would also like to take his eyes, maybe his tongue.

Cassie wanted nothing more and nothing less. She no longer cared about escaping. At the moment, she didn't even really care about getting out of the woods. Gregory was the main reason she wanted out of the woods to begin with.

Jesus, the hunger and paranoia are driving you insane.

She thought this because, standing there, she was actually thinking about going to find Gregory. Seeking him out. She didn't want to kill him, either. She wanted him to go through life bearing all the stigma she wished to bestow upon him, to have a blinding red memento of the day he got paid back.

She wanted to do this because of the way he made her feel, stripping away her pride and dignity and defenses. Everything she had held dear came apart the second she realized she had to get away from him like a hunted animal. The second she realized that, to Gregory, she was no longer human. She could only imagine how she would feel if she had actually been raped.

Maybe infection will slowly rot him away, she thought.

The sound of footsteps pulled her from her musings.

Her heart pounded. Someone had finally found her! She turned her head to try and gauge where the footsteps were coming from. Somewhere off to her left and in front of her. She wanted to run, but it was too dark so she walked cautiously.

Finally, reaching a small clearing, she was able to see her rescuer.

It was Gregory, wandering dazed through the woods, dragging his busted right leg behind him. Cassie cursed herself. She should have known it was him from the broken sound of his walk.

"Cassie!" he called.

Jesus, she thought, *he actually thinks I'm going to answer him.*

She wasn't even sure if he had seen her.

When Gregory stopped, she stood as still as possible, remembering the smallest noise would most possibly be heard.

"Cassie! There's somebody else in the woods!"

Had Gregory been trying to run? Or was he scared? He sounded awfully out of breath.

He stumbled closer to her and she didn't move, too afraid to make a sound.

"Cassie! You stupid fucking bitch! I need help!"

Now he was right in front of her, his side toward her, and she did everything she could to keep from laughing. *Did he actually just ask for help?*

Then he turned toward her and she looked up at him to see if he was looking at her.

He wasn't.

He looked off into the distance and when Cassie looked down at his gut, she saw why.

Something had cut Gregory open. With each exhalation, his intestines bulged out of that opening, threatening to spill down onto his thighs, restrained only by a thin membrane.

Now she didn't think she could help but laugh. *My God, you really have gone insane, laughing at* that?

Then she heard the sound of someone or some*thing* noisily running across the floor of the woods.

She sucked in her breath and tried to make herself as small as possible, the laughter stolen from her throat.

The thing came up on Gregory's blind side and he wasn't able to get away fast enough. The thing bowled Gregory over, driving him to the ground, right next to Cassie.

She stared in awe, too afraid to move.

She had trouble deciphering the thing that hit Gregory. It looked human, except it was larger than the average person. Certain things were pronounced. The arms were long. Its mouth protruded slightly.

It reached down toward Gregory, into Gregory, and pulled out a handful of intestines, gleefully unraveling them. Then it wrapped the intestines around Gregory's neck and squeezed the life out of him. She guessed the fight had gone out of Gregory a long time ago.

Then the thing turned him around, ran a razor sharp claw down his back, laying the skin open, and bent down to feed.

While it did this, Cassie slowly and quietly backed away from it. And while she knew she should probably take this opportunity to run like hell, she didn't think she could do that. She didn't know why exactly. So she continued to scoot back, putting distance and darkness between herself and that thing.

The thing finished feeding and Cassie stopped. It stood up, lifted Gregory off the ground, and slung him over its shoulder before heading back into the woods.

And then, she didn't know why, when all she really should have done was run back the way she had come, she followed that thing to wherever it was going.

It wasn't really true to say she didn't know why she followed it. She knew why. This thing, whatever it was, had killed Gregory much as she had meditated on doing just moments before it happened. She felt she owed it, or him, or whatever, a debt of gratitude. A thank you.

My God, this isn't Beauty and the Beast. *What do you really think you're doing?*

Most of all, it was mysterious. During the past twenty-four hours Cassie had felt as though she'd had all the mysteries of life beaten out of her. By following this monster, she felt like she was reclaiming a little of that mystery.

Nineteen

With a boy of Gregory's girth slung over its shoulders, the thing was able to walk very quickly. Cassie found it difficult to keep up. It was good she didn't have any fear of losing it in a crowd.

It wasn't long before they were out of the woods and into an open field.

She wondered what time it was. Briefly, she contemplated trying to find a road. She now had more a sense of where she was. But that thought was only momentary. She decided something had sent her on this journey, if that's what it was, and it was her job to see the journey through to its end. And that was what she planned to do.

If instincts told her to follow this thing, then follow it she would. It was like she had waited her whole life for something like this to happen. She wasn't about to turn her back on it now. It was insane. The whole scenario was insane. It had been ever since the boom. She didn't think running away was going to make it any more sane.

Besides, she enjoyed watching Gregory's carcass jiggle on the shoulders of that monster.

Still, she continued to think about the craziness. Was it crazy for her to follow this thing that had swiftly disemboweled a childhood "friend" only a few moments ago?

Run with it, she told herself. *You have to.*

But that was just the thing—she *didn't* have to—and that was what made her do it. She was sick of have-tos.

You have to *go to St. Agnes.*

You have to *ride with Gregory.*

You have to *wear that stupid skirt and shirt.*

You have to *run.*

You have to *let Gregory paw you.*

No, she didn't *have to* follow this thing. She *wanted* to. For the first time in a long time, she felt wild and glad to be alive. Just happy to be moving, guided by her own free will and nothing more, racing along in the night, chasing fairy tales.

She lost a lot of ground but if this was the area she was thinking of there weren't anything except open fields and road for probably the next mile. If she could no longer see them, with the quiet stillness, she was sure she would be able to hear them. And she didn't really have any desire to be right up on top of them, anyway.

She continued after them, walking briskly so her leg muscles wouldn't stiffen up. She was glad her boots reached mid-calf so the stiffened, stunted corn didn't scratch her up. Not that she guessed it really mattered much at this point. It would just be another layer of discomfort to add to the growing stack.

Reaching the end of the field, she came to a wire fence. It only reached chest high. The fence had a lot of slack in it. She bent the fence down and climbed over it. From the fence, the meadow in front of her sloped downhill. She saw the huge silhouette of Gregory and the thing off in the distance.

She got close enough to watch the beast set Gregory down by a pond, next to another carcass. This other carcass disturbed her a little more than Gregory's. It made her think maybe she was next. She was willing to take her chances. That would be the capper, wouldn't it? To survive a dangerously massive storm only to be nearly raped. To survive that brutalization only to be killed by something that looked like it came from a horror movie. To be killed only to be eaten.

It's some life you would have led. Most people at least had to live into middle age to survive all of those things, if they're lucky. But you, at the ripe old age of sixteen, could accomplish all of this.

She watched the thing look down at the corpses on the ground, the voice in her head keeping her company. *You can stop thinking of it as a thing. It's definitely a him, even if it is a he-thing. There is nothing feminine about it.*

The voice was right, of course. The voice was almost always right.

She found herself a little more nervous now that the thing wasn't burdened with Gregory. She relaxed when she saw him sit down by the pond. Still, she didn't want to move, didn't want to make any kind of noise. He just sat there and she watched him for an extremely long time. Eventually, he slumped over, most probably asleep, grown sluggish on Gregory's fat.

She went back into the corn a little ways. She figured it might offer her a fraction of camouflage if whatever-the-hell-it-was decided it needed another snack. She lay down, thankful the night was warm and, without wanting to, went to sleep.

Twenty

John awoke with what felt like a massive hangover. True, he'd never drunk or done any type of drug (for some reason, those things seemed to require friends) but it was what he imagined one might feel like. He hovered there in this half-awake, half-dreaming state. He had no idea where he was. He remembered, vaguely, what he had seen down by the road. He remembered running, trying to get away from that hopelessly daunting image of the car just like *melting* into the road.

But where had he run *to*?

He struggled to remember but there was a gap. He couldn't even think of what place had been his intended destination. Not for the first time, he felt a weight pressing down on him. This time, it wasn't any kind of tangible weight, it wasn't anything in the air. He just felt like he was being pulled in too many directions.

He remembered his mother and was seized by the idea, the hope, that she might still be alive somewhere in the rubble of the house.

Yes. Yes. Surely, that was where he had intended to go.

What time was it?

And still, he wondered where he was.

Open your eyes and find out.

Immediately after thinking that, he felt something, something that felt very much like a stick, poke him on the shoulder.

He stood up slowly, brightness clawing at his eyes, and heard a girl say, "You stay right there."

He stood still for a moment, his eyes focusing, adjusting to the light, searching out the voice's owner. Once he got a good look at her, the voice seemed out of place. The girl looked like what he imagined a feral child might look like. She wore a dirty, tattered schoolgirl outfit and untied combat boots that looked way too big for her legs. A crazed look blazed in her eyes. Threateningly, she thrust the stick at him a couple of times.

"I mean it," she said. "Take a step toward me and I'll jab you in the eye."

He didn't know what to say. Until now he'd felt like the victim in all of this, like something God had shit upon. He looked around and noticed another dead body had found its way to the pondside which only added to the now seemingly eternal confusion he'd been feeling.

"Who are you?" the girl demanded.

"Wait," he said, his body swooning, his brain overloaded. "I just… I'm… think I'm going to sit back down." And he did.

He took the time to look around and orient himself. It was dawn. The ground was still covered in fog. He took a deep breath of the clean moisture. He now knew what time it was, where he was. Now he just needed it to all click somewhere inside of his head.

"Who are you?" she demanded again.

"Well, my name's John Fresk. I live here. Who are you?" He crisscrossed his legs in front of him and leaned over them, rocking slightly.

"You're not the thing I saw last night," she said.

"I've never seen you until just now." He realized that when two confused people have a conversation, each one assumes the other is insane.

"I know, but I saw you. I followed you here."

"Where did you follow me from?" He felt like he was humoring a senile old lady. He also felt like this girl could, quite possibly, color in the empty spaces he couldn't manage for himself.

"The woods."

"I don't remember going into the woods. I was trying to get to the house. When did you follow me here?"

"Last night. Just after dark."

"I must have been sleepwalking."

"You weren't sleepwalking."

"Okay… Would *you* like to tell me what I was doing?"

"You brought *him* back here." She jabbed her stick at the fat, mostly naked corpse.

"Did I? And who is that?"

"That's Gregory. I went to school with him."

"Are you the one that did… *that* to him?"

"No. You are."

John almost laughed. "Yeah, okay. I guess I killed my dad, too, huh?"

"Oh my God, that's your dad?"

"Yeah." John couldn't bear to look at him. "Would you like to tell me *how* I killed him? I'm not really the violent type."

"Last night, when you didn't look like you do now, you gutted him and then you choked him with his guts."

He grimaced. "What do you mean, 'When I didn't look like I do now'?"

"You were different."

"How was I different?"

"You were bigger. And you had like big claws or something…"

"Like a monster?"

"*Exactly* like a monster."

"And I killed *him*. And you followed me here?"

"Yes."

"Why did you follow me here?"

"I was glad you killed him. He was the real monster. I wanted to say thank you."

"Is he the reason you look like that?"

"Yeah, pretty much."

"So you were in the woods with him?"

"I was running from him. During the storm."

"Yeah, the storm." Memories of the past couple days came back to him. He stood up. "I'm glad you're here," he said. "Things have been really weird since the storm."

"That's an understatement."

"Everything's dead."

"Not us." It came out as a near whisper, like she didn't completely believe it.

"What's *your* name, by the way?"

"Cassie Duvall. I live in town but I go to St. Agnes in Milltown."

"Okay. Well, anyway, everything's not dead everywhere. And I don't think we're able to leave. There's like a force field or something around us."

"I'll need to leave."

"Yeah, I'm sure you will. You must have been in the woods before the boom."

"The boom knocked me out."

"Me too. Anyway, yesterday, I tried to get help, but I couldn't because I couldn't leave, you know? And then I went down to the road to see if any cars were passing thinking maybe they would see me and know I needed help or something but I ended up seeing things I didn't want to see and then I just got sick of it all and took off running. I don't know where the hell I was going. And then, I don't know, I guess I just decided to take a nap or something. I was exhausted. It was... hard to walk. Will you help me?"

"Help you with what?"

"It looks like the storm or the boom or something knocked our house down. I think my mother might be in there somewhere. If she didn't make it to the cellar then she's dead, but if she's in the cellar then she should be alive. Will you help me get her out? If we can find the refrigerator, there should be some food in there."

"Okay, but you lead the way."

"You'll help me?"

"Yeah, sure, but the second you try anything. *Any*thing, even a strange look, I'm gone."

"Oh, you mean like if I try and eat you?"

"Exactly."

"Sounds fair. Can I ask you something?"

"What?"

"Why do you want to help me?"

"I have my reasons."

"Well, then thank you, I guess."

John stood up and led the way over to the house, thinking it was nice to have a companion.

Twenty-one

It didn't take them long to reach the house. Cassie trailed about three feet behind the entire way, brandishing the stick in front of her. At one point, John came to a stop and said, "Will you put down the stick?"

"I can't do that," was her reply.

"You *really* don't need it."

"Maybe I should just go. Would you rather I do that?"

"No, please. Okay, if the stick makes you feel better."

"It does."

"Fine."

"And you better sound happy about it!" She waggled the stick ferociously to show him she meant business.

"Great! I love the stick!" He smiled a big, false smile that immediately disappeared from his face.

"That's what I like to hear."

Christ, he thought.

Once at the house the destruction was more obvious. It was, quite literally, leveled. Even the foundation that, at its highest point, came up to John's thigh, was shattered and crumbled. It looked more like an earthquake had struck it than a tornado. And, if it *had* been a tornado, it had been unseen by John.

"Do you think a tornado could have done that?" he asked.

"I didn't see a tornado. Don't remember hearing anything about one either. I mean, like on the radio or anything before the storm."

"I didn't either. Of course, I was pretty much outside when the storm hit."

"Yeah, me too but, I don't know, doesn't look like a tornado."

"No. Definitely not. Oh, by the way, that used to be my house."

"My God," she said. "Your mom's in *there*?"

"Well, hopefully she got out. Or made it down into the cellar."

But, at this point, he wasn't even sure how safe the cellar could possibly be. The majority of the rocks that made up the house had fallen neatly inward, forming a kind of pyramid. A number of other rocks had been cast out, lying around the bulk of the house in a crude circle. They were going to have to remove a lot more rocks then he had hoped. If the house had exploded outward or to any side besides the north side, where the cellar was located, they could have quickly removed the rocks. Now, however, they were going to have to start removing the rocks at the top of the pyramid until they got to nearly the bottom layer.

And then there was the whole matter of food. The refrigerator was down there somewhere, beneath all the rocks. If it had not exploded on impact, much of the food would still be edible. This was one instance where the rocks might actually be beneficial, keeping the sun and the elements away from the food.

Right now, he wanted a drink more than anything. If the weather yesterday was any indication about today (and in Ohio, that wasn't always the case) it would once again be blisteringly hot.

As if mimicking his thoughts, Cassie said, "Jesus. I'm thirsty as fuck."

He nodded and thought for a moment. "There's a well over by the side of the house. The water that comes out of it's pretty good, but we'll need something to hold it in… and something to lower it with."

"You know the place better than I do," she said, raking her hair back and curling it around her ear. The ear was pale flesh, sharply contrasting with the dirt on her face.

"Let me think," he said.

He started walking around the house, looking here and there. The flowerpots had holes in the bottom. One of the birdhouses might work. But where the hell was he going to find a rope? Maybe in one of the cars' trunks, but the keys were most assuredly in the house. He cursed his parents for being so routine. They always hung their keys on a letter holder suspended on the wall beside the phone. They religiously locked their cars because, as his father always said, "You never know who passes through the dark country while we're asleep."

While following him, Cassie asked, "Why aren't you in there?"

"I guess, by all rights, I should be."

"But you're not."

"I guess I was feeling suicidal. I don't know. I wanted to stay out in the storm. You know, feel its power or whatever. Does that sound gay?"

"No, it sounds stupid. Were you really... suicidal?"

"No. Just bored, I guess."

Then John had an idea.

There was an old tire swing hanging from the Chinese elm tree at the front of the house. He remembered trying to ride it as a child and how the water that collected in it always got his ass wet. And, of course, it came equipped with its very own rope.

"Follow me," he said.

Together, they finished walking around to the front of the house. Now, exactly how were they supposed to get it down? It didn't hang that high off the ground so they *could* try untying it. Or they could try and break the branch off. That would probably be the easiest way. Or they could cut it down. But that would take a knife and they didn't have a knife.

At least, *he* didn't have a knife.

"Hey," he said. "You have a knife?"

"If I did, I probably wouldn't need this stick," she said.

"You don't need the stick anyway."

"You didn't see what I saw."

"What was it that you saw again?"

"I already told you."

"No. You said, back by the pond, that I didn't look the way I did last night. Or something like that. You told me a few other things but I still don't know what you meant."

Maybe, John thought, by asking her about it when she wasn't thinking of an answer, he could catch her in a lie. Because he really didn't want to believe he was a murderer, least of all a patricidalist.

"The thing I saw last night. *You*. Didn't look like you do now. I mean, he looked kind of like you. He was wearing the same clothes you're wearing. But he was bigger—uglier. Kind of like an ape, but not hairy. You had a lot of teeth. And they were big. *Huge*. Your arms were really long and you had big sharp claws. That's what you used to gore Gregory. And you were obviously very strong. I mean, you carried him from all the way back in the woods to the pond and he must weigh like close to 300 pounds. The fat fucking pig."

"So he was a good friend?"

"I wouldn't go that far."

"So, if I was huge and tall, like you said, and I was wearing the same clothes, why aren't they stretched or ripped or something?"

"Look how baggy your fucking clothes are. You look like a skinny kid who shops in the fat kid section."

"Thanks."

"Besides, you were big, but it wasn't like Incredible Hulk big. I mean, you were mostly taller."

"And why aren't my clothes covered in blood?"

"Well, let's see," Cassie said. "Black shirt and, I don't know, those shorts look pretty stained. Kind of like they *used* to be some kind of color."

"I've been sleeping outside the past two nights."

"Do you want to smell the stains? I imagine old blood has a different smell than mud."

"I think I'll pass on that. And why were *you* outside during the storm?"

"I'm getting pretty sick of your fucking questions. I'm the one with the stick, remember?"

"So why didn't I kill you, too?"

"I don't know. Maybe you were saving the best for last." Then she brandished the stick at him again and shouted, "Stick!"

"Cute."

"So why do you need a knife, anyway?"

He gestured toward the tire swing. She didn't seem as impressed with him as he was with himself.

"So," she said. "You like to make swinging more dangerous, or what?"

He laughed and said, "No, see, it collects water there at the bottom. We can lower it into the well."

"Great. I get to drink out of an old tire. I already feel like a princess."

"If you're as thirsty as me, you'd drink your own piss. That is if you had enough body fluids left to manufacture piss."

"Lovely," she said. "So how we gonna get it down?"

"I dunno."

He stalked up to the tire. "Maybe I can just break the branch off. This tree's pretty old and brittle."

He wrapped his hands around the dirty yellow rope and hung from it, bouncing up and down. The branch barely gave. His father had done a good job in picking out the safest one, he guessed.

"How hard do you think it would be to untie it?" she asked.

"Probably not too hard. I imagine it's just your standard slipknot. Maybe a little crusted over. But one of us would have to get up there."

"Oh, that's not a problem," she said.

She went over to the tree trunk and, grabbing onto some lower branches, had herself up to the swing's branch in no time.

"That was impressive," he called.

"Thank you," she said. She sat down on the branch, her back to John since she had suddenly become conscious of the fact she didn't have any underwear on, and scooted her way out toward the knot.

Tensely, he watched her, expecting her to fall off at any moment. "Be careful," he said.

She reached the knot and bent over it, her fingers struggling with it.

"I wish I had your fingers," she laughed.

"Probably wouldn't help much," he said. "I've managed to avoid manual labor all my life."

"Not the farmer type, huh?"

"Far from it."

He watched her arms shake with the effort. The morning fog had burnt off and it was starting to heat up.

"So you really can't get off this land?" she asked.

"You can see for yourself when you get down."

Then he remembered how the corn was all dead, but alive on the other side of the imaginary line.

"Actually, from where you are, look out toward the field. You see how the corn is brown and dead but only up to a certain point? That's the line I couldn't cross."

"That doesn't look right," she said.

"It isn't."

"Got it," she said right before the tire thunked down into the scorched grass.

"Now how you gonna get down?" he called.

"I have my ideas," she said.

She continued to scoot to the end of the branch, bending under her weight the farther out she went. "Too bad that won't get us enough water to take a bath. I feel rancid."

"You could always throw yourself down the well. Nothing

would get a camera crew out here faster than that."

"Maybe that's not a bad idea. Why hasn't there been anyone here?"

"I was wondering that same thing earlier. The only thing I could imagine was that everyone has had a rough time of it. My dad worked for the reserve and they haven't even been by. I think other things are happening too. I mean, I don't think it's just that we can't get out. I don't think anyone would be able to come in either. Hell, maybe everything looks *normal* from out there. I really just don't know much about anything anymore."

While John spoke, Cassie continued working her way to the end of the branch.

She waited until it levitated about eight feet from the ground before finally hopping off, holding the front and back of her skirt down with both hands.

She dusted off her hands and said, "My mother always told me I would get myself killed doing that. But I might have just kept us from dying of thirst."

"Bravo," John said, clapping his hands. "You did much better than I could have. I don't think I've ever climbed a tree."

"Why don't you show me to this fucking well," she said.

He picked up the tire and led her in a semicircle around to the back corner of the house.

A three-by-three cement square rose up from the grass, a small plank wood door lying across it.

He pulled the door off and said proudly, "There it is."

She leaned her head into it and said, "Mmm, I never thought I would describe water as smelling delicious, but it truly does."

John wiped the scummy inside of the tire out with his shirttail and said, "This comes straight from an underground spring, too. People would pay a dollar a bottle for this stuff."

Cassie laughed. "I think it has to come from Canada or Maine or something. Maybe France."

"Yeah. Do you think people know that those are the places that get our acid rain?"

"Just get some water, would you?"

He lowered the tire, almost expecting the well to be empty. It wouldn't have surprised him at all. The sound of the rubber splashing into the cool water sent a welcome wave of relief throughout his body. He brought the tire up and sat it down in the grass. She got down on all fours and, before hungrily lapping it up with her tongue, said, "I could use a straw."

"No, water's meant to be drank right from the rubber. That's how I always thought about it."

Cassie stood up and said, "It's all yours, tiger."

Twenty-two

Both their thirsts slaked, Cassie said, "You ready to find your mom?"

John looked at the huge mound of stone and said, "I'm not even sure she's worth it."

Cassie didn't laugh.

"Joking," he said.

"Good time for it. Really appropriate."

John didn't laugh.

"Joking," she said.

"Not funny," he said, joking.

Together, they climbed the pile of stones. It felt like a mountain.

The sun was already straight overhead, beating down on them, shining up at them from the lightly colored stone. It suddenly occurred to John that this was going to take a very long time. The simple climb to the top had caused all of his muscles to go rubbery. Already, the only thing he could really think about was finding a cool place to sleep. A wave of regret washed over him. Confusion or not, he felt like he *really* should have started yesterday.

"We might be working on this come dawn tomorrow," he said.

"Huh-uh," Cassie said. "We need to talk about some things."

He grabbed the first rock and tossed it. Or, rather, he *rolled* it, giving it enough momentum to go tumbling off the pile and into the grass. "Whaddya mean?"

Cassie grunted and rolled a stone down the opposite side. "Well, if the theory that I've got about you is true, then I have no intention of being around you come dark."

"And what's this theory?" Another rock went chunking down.

Cassie took a deep breath, fastening her hands to her hips and fixing him with a bitter stare. "Despite the two dead bodies over there by the pond, you still seem to be oblivious to the fact that it was you who put them there."

He avoided her stare, overconcentrating on the rocks below him, chucking another one down the pile.

"I'm sorry that I don't see myself as a murderer."

"Well *I* do. I *saw* you murder. Even if I hated the stupid pigfucker it happened to, I *saw* you do it. And you did it without any reasons whatsoever. You *killed* Gregory."

"Yes, you've made that clear."

She hurled a rock down the pile, mad. Then she refixed her hands to her hips, the burn of her stare increased, the huff of her voice a little louder. "Look, if you think I'm a fucking lunatic, then just say so! But I *know* what I saw and I'm here, trying to help you. So if you want to just dismiss everything I say, then fine, I can go back over there and lay down by the pond or try and figure out a way to get the fuck out of here rather than stand here and help you try to find your mommy."

John realized he'd been somewhat of an ass. He stopped his intense movement of the rocks and looked at her.

"Okay," he said. "I don't want anything to happen to you… And I appreciate that you're helping me. Maybe the best thing to do is to find some kind of solution. We're in this together."

"For better or worse."

"To say the least. By the way, can things *get* any worse?"

"Yes, for me, *tonight*, if we don't figure something out. You said you can't leave this area. Before dark, I need to find out if *I* can. If I could leave, then maybe I could go find help. But, out of three people besides yourself that were trapped in this area, that aren't buried under stone, two of them are dead. It stands to reason that I'll be next."

"Do you have any ideas?"

"Well, I thought I could barricade myself somewhere safe and that you would be able to satiate yourself with animals or what have you…"

"There don't seem to be any of those. All of the fish and frogs in the pond, if you didn't notice, seem to be kind of dead, and I haven't heard a single bird—which is *really* strange out here."

"Nevertheless, the idea is to keep you from getting to me. Ideally, I would like to restrain *you* and see exactly what it is that happens to you and when."

"What makes you think it has to be dark before I change? I mean, you said it was like I 'satiate' myself on the corpses. Maybe I change into it as soon as the hunger starts."

"Are you trying to scare me more than I already am?"

"No. Sorry. I'm just… trying to make sure all of our bases are covered."

"So we need to think about finding some way to restrain or barricade you. If we can get this dug away by nightfall, I mean, we still have a lot of time, then we could put you in the cellar and pile rocks on it or fucking park a car on it or something."

"I don't think that's going to happen."

"What's not going to happen?"

"A couple of things, really. One, the keys to the cars are buried somewhere in this rubble. My parents always hang theirs in the same spot and I distinctly remember throwing mine on my dresser. Second, there's no way in hell that we are going to get this rubble cleared away by nightfall."

"I don't know. We're making pretty good progress."

"That has nothing to do with it. The days are fucked up."

"How's that?"

"I don't know, exactly. But yesterday, well, it just wasn't as long as a day in June should be, even before the time change. Didn't you notice?"

"No. I was in the woods and…"

"And what?"

"Nothing."

"Okay." He didn't want to stress her or make her any more uncomfortable. He already sensed something bad had happened between her and Gregory.

"Anyway, so I guess we need to think of another way to restrain you."

"There's the rope."

"I don't know if that'll be strong enough. Certainly not strong enough for me to sit around and watch what happens to you."

"Okay, well, what else is there?"

She had another idea, but she didn't want to tell him, afraid his knowledge might carry over into his other state.

They continued throwing stones. In this heat, it was probably the worst place they could be. Sweat dripped off both of them. Silently, they worked away, each of them thinking about their curious fates and about the potentially hazardous fate awaiting Cassie.

Paranoia nagged at John as he realized his fate could be as hazardous as Cassie's. Given the fears she professed to him, he had every right to be as suspicious of her as she was of him. It *was* possible she had murdered his father and that fat kid who was in the pasture. It was also possible he did it. If that was the case and she *knew* it was the case, he had reason to believe she had every reason to want to off him before nightfall. Even if he was the killer, he didn't think he should have to die for something he had no control over.

He imagined himself bent over, Cassie driving a heavy rock onto his skull.

The more he thought about it, the more he thought that maybe she *was* the murderer. Or else why didn't she kill him when he was asleep—unless what she said about wanting to thank him was true. If so, she must *really* hate that guy.

He didn't really know of a way to broach his disbelief that he was unquestionably the killer. That thought seemed to make her pretty mad and he couldn't risk offending her. If his mother was still alive then he needed Cassie's help. Because if his mother was down there it meant she'd been down there for coming up on 48 hours and John didn't know how long it would take insanity or hunger to claim her. He figured insanity would probably come first.

Cassie spoke, breaking his thought. "I'm going to go down and get some more water. Coming?"

"Sure," he rasped.

Twenty-three

Over by the well, they began the water ceremony, each of them taking turns drinking from the tire like a dog from a dish.

Wiping some water from her dirty chin, Cassie said, "I've been thinking. One of those cars over there is yours?" She motioned over to the three cars lined up in the driveway, the ability to park straight seemingly not bestowed upon the Fresk family.

"Yeah, the shitty one."

"Are the doors locked?"

"They should be… But they might not be." He vaguely remembered having a notion of leaving it unlocked, thinking he might go back out after the storm. Sometimes he liked to drive around and survey the damage. "We could go check, I guess."

"It might not be necessary. You don't have the keys, right?"

"Definitely not."

"Does your car have one of those automatic trunks? That you can operate from the inside?"

"Yeah. The gas tank's like that too."

"Oh, very modern," Cassie smirked. "Could you fit in the trunk?"

"Sure. Wouldn't be very comfortable."

"And this is?" Cassie motioned to everything around them.

"Good point."

"Let's go see if it's unlocked. If so, that's where you'll be sleeping tonight."

He wasn't sure if he wanted to do that. If she were a murderess, this would be the perfect opportunity for her to trap him. He wasn't even really afraid of what might happen. He just didn't want to feel like a dupe. Even though he honestly felt like she knew what she was talking about, there was still a part of him that wanted to be the innocent one in this whole thing.

He guessed he finally had to bring it up.

"Let's talk about this," he said, leading her toward the car.

"It's the best thing I can think of. Do you have any big ideas?"

"Why don't *you* get in the trunk?"

"Be*cause*, if it has one of those automatic thingies, then you could easily use it and get at me. I said you were a beast, I didn't say you were dumb."

She had missed his point entirely, but only for a second. He didn't have to say anything else.

"Oh my *God*," she said. "You *still* don't believe it was you, do you?"

She turned away from the direction of the car, toward the road.

"Well, fuck you!" she spat. "How do I know you're not lying to *me*? After seeing what you do at night, I shouldn't even be here! I have no *reason* to trust you. You're probably just trying to keep me here so you *can* have a feast at night!"

He bemusedly watched as she stalked down the driveway. He was interested to see if she could get through the invisible wall. Hell, he hoped she *did*. While watching her, he absent-mindedly opened his car door. Yep, unlocked. If, he thought, he *really* wanted to avoid going into the trunk, he could have, then and there, locked the doors and told Cassie, "Sorry, looks like we'll have to find another way."

He looked at the little lock switch, depressed in the inside of the door, the little neon orange stripe warning him the door was unlocked. *I could just flip that*, he thought. But he doubted himself as much as he did Cassie. Probably more.

When he looked back at her, squinting his eyes against the huge sun already sliding down the western sky, he saw that she was on the ground. Should he go help her or stay back and hope she'd learned her lesson?

He thought of his mother, trapped beneath all those stones. The sooner they could get her out, the better. The gravel crunched beneath his tennis shoes as he went down to Cassie.

She wasn't getting up.

His legs like jelly, he managed to step his pace up to a trot in order to reach her. Once beside her, he grabbed her by the arms and pulled her up.

Blood trickled from her nose, slathering the dark crust already gathered around her nostrils. Her eyes rolled back into her head.

"Cassie," he said, shaking her.

Her eyes—a beautiful green, he realized for the first time—bounced up and down.

"Cassie, dammit!"

He shook her again.

She made a sound like, "Muh…"

He let go of her to see if she could stand. Momentarily, she kept her balance and then drooped to her knees, folding her torso over her thighs and covering the back of her head with her arms.

She mumbled something.

He bent down to her level. "What?"

"Shade. Think I need some shade."

"Can you walk?"

She moaned. "I guess if I have to."

He thought about his morning's work of lugging the stones and, thinking it might have the same effect as using a fungo bat in baseball, bent to put his left arm behind her back. She threw her right arm around his neck, and he pulled her up.

"Here goes," he said. She couldn't weigh much more than one of the big rocks. He put his right arm in the crook behind her knees and pulled her off her feet. Her skirt slid up her thighs and she quickly pushed it down in between her legs with her free hand.

"You'll be okay," he said.

He took her to an old oak in the backyard and laid her down on the shady side, dead leaves clinging to the branches, before leaving to get her some water.

He returned, placing the tire of fresh water down next to her head. She leaned over to groggily sip the water and then asked him to pour it on her. He did so. It was then, after the water had taken away some of the dirt and muck from her face that he saw how beautiful she was. He realized suddenly that he should feel honored to have exchanged any words at all with this girl. He sat down cross-legged beside her and put his hand to her forehead, relishing the heat emanating from her.

"You're all right," he said.

"I don't really think you're a monster," she mumbled. "But we have to be careful, you know?"

"Rest, Cassie."

"I hope your mom's alive."

"Me, too."

"I'm glad Gregory's dead."

"If it makes you happy, then I am too."

"We've got to make the most of this."

"You need to rest. I'm going to go do some more digging. Don't try and move a lot, okay?"

"Will you stay in the trunk tonight?"

He didn't want to say yes but he looked into her drowsy green eyes, caught a glimmer of what her skin would be like if it weren't filthed up and said, "Yes."

He would spend the rest of the afternoon trying to convince himself he'd made the right choice.

Twenty-four

John made decent progress on the pile of stones, but it was still little more than half-depleted by the time the sun was almost out of the sky. *This is useless*, he thought.

He didn't know how he was going to be able to go at this alone. What was the point in continuing if he wasn't going to be able to finish? If his mother was still going to be left down there to rot? *Tomorrow*, he told himself. Tomorrow they would have to work faster and harder. After all, what else were they going to do? The only important things right now were food and his mother's freedom. He probably didn't even need food, if everything Cassie said was true, but *she* had to be starving. Grimly, he wondered if they would have to resort to cannibalism. Water from a tire and some meat from his father. How palatable.

He had unofficially diagnosed Cassie with heat exhaustion and, despite her attempts to get up and join him, he demanded that she rest. He convinced himself that his mother, if still alive, would be all right for another day. Besides, the way things were looking, he figured she might be safer in the basement than around here. That was all she needed. To be rescued from a suffocating death only to be eaten by her hideous monster of a child. He was tired of thinking all these ridiculous thoughts. None of them were good, he knew and, the more he worked, the worse the thoughts were going to get.

He threw off another stone and decided to call that the last one of the day. Tentatively, he climbed down the stones that had once made up the house.

While descending, he looked at Cassie, sleeping in the grass. He couldn't help but see her as some kind of holy grail. Maybe she could make his black thoughts go away for a fraction of a second, at least.

Reaching her, he stood over her for a moment. It felt like voyeurism. She was so beautiful, he felt guilty for ogling her. He nudged her with his shoe.

"Wake up, sleepyhead."

She groggily opened her eyes and he could tell she still hadn't gotten all the rest she needed. Once all the way opened, there was still a foggy lack of recognition in her eyes.

"It's almost dark," he said. And then, somewhat ruefully, "It's time for me to get in the trunk."

She stood up. She had almost sweated her mask of filth away.

"Is it dark already?"

"Damn near. I didn't want to take any chances. How did you want to go about doing this?"

She rubbed sleep from her eyes and yawned, still gathering her bearings. Maybe she had lost her plan altogether, he thought. Maybe this was all some terrible nightmare and he could spend the night by her side, sleeping under the clear night sky and waiting for all the nightmares to curl up and die. "Well," she finally said. "I figured we should probably tie you up with the rope. You know, really hogtie you, and then put you in the trunk. I'll get you out at the first sign of dawn."

"And if I'm not the killer? I mean, will you be okay? I mean, what if there's somebody *else* lurking around here? Or... or what if it doesn't have anything to do with day and night. What if it has to do with how hungry I am, like you said earlier? If I need to feed and can't find any food, what makes you think I'll be good old John come morning?"

"Well, I'd put my money on you. I definitely don't think there's anyone else wandering around here. I'll be careful opening the trunk in the morning. I'll get an even bigger stick. I'll tap on the trunk and make sure that it's you in there."

"But how will you know that?"

"Because you won't sound so full of teeth, I imagine."

"Are you absolutely *sure* there wouldn't be anybody else it could be?"

"I'm not absolutely sure of anything anymore. This is your land. Does anybody else live on it?"

"No. I mean, I think we're it as far as the quarantine or whatever the fuck you want to call it goes." He pointed to the east. "I don't know how far back that way it goes but, based on the distance from the sides that we do know about, I don't think it reaches any residences or anything. It's mostly just the reserve back there, anyway."

"Well, then that means the only other person it could be would be me. In which case, I should ask, will *you* be okay?"

"I think so. Just in case, maybe we should forego the rope. There are some things in the trunk, the tire jack and all, that I could use to defend myself. If a car trunk won't hold me, then I don't really think the rope would do any good, do you?"

"Good point. We can forget about the rope." She looked at the orange ball of sun almost visibly sliding down into the dark horizon. "The way it looks, we might not have enough time to do you up right, anyway."

They stood awkwardly for a few moments, stealing glances at one another when they knew the other one wasn't looking. It was times like these John hated himself for being so shy and pensive. He wanted to grab her and tell her how scared he was and that he knew she was scared and that he would do anything in his power to make sure nothing would ever hurt her. Instead, he merely stood there, alternately looking at her and the gravel of the driveway.

"All right, then," she said. "I guess we should put you in that trunk."

"I guess." He shuffled over to the car.

Cassie opened the door, reached down, and popped the trunk, John staring at the lean musculature of her legs. Before she could rise up and catch him gawking at her, he moved his head, staring at the confining darkness of the trunk.

"Good thing I'm not claustrophobic."

"Think of it as cozy." She patted him on the back. Her touch sent shivers of pleasure across his skin.

He hesitated before getting in. Then he turned to her and said, "I really hope we're right. I hope there's not… something else out here. I meant it when I said I didn't want anything to happen to you."

"That's nice. I can take care of myself. Really. Everything'll be okay and tomorrow we can find your mom. That's all we can let ourselves think about right now."

"I hope so," he said, stepping up into the trunk. Once he arranged himself so his body fit, he said, "Go ahead."

"See you in the morning." She pulled the trunk closed, bringing night upon John's day very quickly.

Panic twinged through his body. As soon as the door was closed, he wanted out. Now he knew why claustrophobics were claustrophobic. But he bit back the yell that so desperately wanted to surface.

There was only the dark, he told himself, trying not to think about the small space.

Only dark.

Only dark.

Twenty-five

Soon after being confined to the trunk, John's legs and neck ached and he wished he had chosen a different way to lie. He was in the fetal position, his knees nearly pressing against the trunk door, digging into them. It made it impossible to think about anything other than his discomfort. Perhaps if he had chosen to put his knees against the back of the seat, he wouldn't be so incredibly uncomfortable. After moving rocks all day, he should be stretched out right now, not curled up into a ball. Already, he braced himself for the pain he knew he would feel in the morning.

The fear for his safety had completely vanished. He knew he was the killer. It had to be him. For one thing, it would explain a lot. Like his gaps in memory over the past two nights. Like why he didn't get hungry during the day. Like why he found himself looking forward to the night, salivating like Pavlov's dogs and how he had to try so hard and keep that a secret from Cassie. How he was almost glad she had been virtually unconscious the past couple of hours. How he didn't really know if what he felt when near her was desire or hunger. Like how he could be so uncomfortable and still so very tired.

It just seemed easier if he was the killer. They had already planned for that. They had already protected themselves against it. Otherwise, it meant somebody else was the killer. Maybe somebody who had been watching them all day. Plotting against them. Listening to them. Trying to find ways to make their fear work against them. And if there *was* someone else out there, John didn't know how the hell he was ever going to get out of the trunk. And if someone, the killer, did come to let him out of the trunk, he couldn't really see how the outcome could be all that good. The only good thing that could come from someone else being the killer was the relief that would be placed on his conscience.

He didn't know how long these thoughts went on, swirling around on themselves like storm clouds, the next thought more ludicrous and terrifying than the previous one. But they continued, a dread backbeat lurking like heat lightning in the storm clouds. He wanted out of the trunk. He wanted out of his head. He wanted off all this tainted land. He wanted Cassie. He wanted food.

Soon the lightning and the thoughts sank away, the deeper, foggier darkness of unconsciousness beckoning to him. He didn't see how sleep was possible but it infested itself behind his eyes, making his head feel heavy, infusing him with the sense that he was floating, leaving his body.

Maybe this is how it works without coffee or Pepsi, he thought.

It was the last thought he had that night.

Effortlessly, he drifted out onto the dark river, floating into a place where his dreams were not allowed, his essential being leaving with his consciousness, ready to be filled with something else entirely.

Twenty-six

After leaving the car, Cassie went over to the well to get some more water. It was best to keep as many fluids in as possible. Pulling the old tire up toward her, she hadn't realized how heavy an old tire full of water could be. Her arms shook as she tugged at the rough old rope. She took a drink and thought about how she longed for a shower. Not a bath. That would be too much like sitting in her own filth. No, she wanted to feel the hot water beating against her skin, scraping the dirt and blood and piss from her body and carrying it down the drain to the sewer where it belonged.

She finished the water and, seeing that it had served her well all day, chose the old oak tree as her place of respite.

Sleep would be impossible. She knew that.

She sat down in the last fingers of the dying sun and thought about how she *should* be scared shitless. But she wasn't. It was probably just a combination of fatigue, frayed nerves, and lingering shock. Whatever it was, it was fantastic. Some layer of unreality had settled over her ever since the incident with Gregory at the dam. There were things she never thought would happen to her. There were depths she didn't think people from her sane suburban world delved into. She had discovered very quickly exactly how wrong all of her assumptions were. So now her perceptions were skewed. She didn't know if that was a good thing or a bad thing.

She lay there and thought about survival.

Maybe that was what it came down to. Survival was the raw essential, wasn't it? Each person had a different definition of survival but, nevertheless, it defined who they were. Most people did what they did, on a daily basis, just to get by—either physically or mentally. So, whoever she had become, whoever she was there under the oak tree, that was her essential self. There was something about that thought she liked. She saw herself as sympathetic and helpful and surprisingly calm. She liked herself. And she felt more grown up than she ever had before. Grown up and still so full of dreams.

She imagined John and herself living in a kind of paradise where all that was dead became alive and they could wander around on this paradise searching for the next bite of food or their next fantasy.

But some bit of practicality stopped her from exploring this dream too far. They were still in a bad situation. No amount of dreaming could change that. If anything, the dreaming would only make the reality that much harsher.

She looked over at the house, or what had been the house, silhouetted black against the horizon. She thought about how hard John must have worked to tear that much away. Given the circumstances, she guessed she would have done the same thing.

It was hard to imagine there might be a human buried somewhere in there. Of course, it was hard to imagine there were two dead bodies lying over by the pond. It was hard to imagine she'd almost been raped. Even the incident with Gregory at the dam and the storm that followed were hard to imagine. It all seemed so far away.

It was just some kind of crazy test, she thought. She wondered why her journey into womanhood had to be so violent. Maybe every girl's was, in varying degrees.

The journey wasn't over. She knew that. Sitting there, she was still just a sad girl beneath an old oak tree. And as harsh as that far away reality seemed she could never be aware of how bad things were going to get.

For the first time since it had all started, the heaviness wrenched her heart, tearing at it, shoving it to the back of her body where it welled up in her mind and forced out tears.

It was much needed.

The comfort she had felt only moments before dissipated completely. This was good, she thought. Comfort only bred complacency. She could not let herself become complacent. Here, complacency would probably mean death and she could not let herself begin walking the path that lead to death. She had to stay alive as much for John as herself.

Twilight darkened into night and she sat there, shaking with the force of her sobs, letting all the anger and frustration build up inside her, giving her the ferocious strength she could never have otherwise.

Twenty-seven

In the trunk of the car, John stirred. But not yet with consciousness. He, John, wouldn't know consciousness for quite some time. But there was something in him stirring his makeup, changing his composition to better suit its needs. His teeth multiplied. His fingers lengthened, thickened. His nails hardened and grew long and sharp. His muscles swelled, augmented, became powerful.

Within the musty confines of the trunk, he breathed as deeply as he could. All the smells of the devastated night reached into his brain, into his viscera.

He smelled the scent of death—the dead grass, the dead trees and the richer, cloyingly sweet rot of the dead things by the pond. Yes, it was the smell the Johnthing relished, but it was not a smell he craved.

He knew the smells he craved and knew there were two of them. He attached importance to them, but couldn't figure out why either of them was important. These other things he smelled, these things he craved, he craved because of the life that clung to them. It was the life he wanted to feast upon. It was these people, these things, these *creatures* he wanted to open up and it was this life he wanted to drain from them. He was just a vessel, this he knew, *felt* deep down, and he knew all the life he could ingest would make him stronger, would further the cause, increase his standing. Tonight, he would take one of those creatures that smelled so full of life and turn it into that other thing, the dead thing, that he would relish tomorrow.

The scent of a dead thing was like a piece of art. Something to be merely observed and never touched. Something that deepened and gained meaning over time through no action save that of age and decomposition.

Tonight, he wanted the young one. The freshest one that threatened to burst like a piece of ripened fruit. Through scent alone, the Johnthing could feel how the blood pounded through her veins, charging from her heart. He wanted to feel the blood splash around in his mouth, become infested in his veins and wash over his skin. That was his singular desire. It was impossible to think about anything else. Even though there was a part of him that knew what he was doing was part of something greater there was another part of him, a part sunk way down deep inside of him, the part that swam in a dark dream world, the part that knew what he was doing was wrong *so wrong*, he still couldn't think about anything other than the ripping of skin and the fountain of blood.

Tonight he would feast.

Tonight. Tonight.

His thoughts did not range any further than this night, this now.

John's arm shot out straight in front of him, creasing the steel of the trunk.

He sensed the scent nearby and rammed both arms into the lid, its lock already threatening to give way.

This wasn't going to be a challenge at all.

He would have his feast.

Tonight.

Twenty-eight

Cassie heard the initial metallic bending of the car's trunk and was immediately on her feet. Although she was slightly curious as to whether or not John could make it out of the trunk, she had no desire to stick around.

It looked like she was going to have to utilize her other plan, the one she had neglected to tell John about.

It wasn't a pretty plan and she really didn't even know why it should work. But in a world that no longer made sense, she felt like every notion should be explored.

She knew there wouldn't be any hiding from John.

There certainly couldn't be any running. After all, there didn't seem to be any place *to* run.

The second time John hit the trunk, just a few seconds after the first, sounded even more forceful, more... *productive.*

Cassie took off running toward the pond, resisting the urge to veer off and run as far back into the woods as possible.

The blood pounding in her ears and the crunch of her boots on the gravel and then the dead grass made it impossible to think, let alone hear, anything.

She hit the field and kept running toward the pond.

Once at the pond, standing between those two dead bodies, she heard a sound like a car crash.

That was probably it, she figured.

She didn't look forward to what she was going to do. She didn't hesitate either.

John roared and it cut through the night.

God, I hope this works.

Cassie straddled Gregory, sitting on his upper thighs, and reached down into the wound John had made. She grabbed a flank of skin with each hand and pulled until she split him apart, cringing at the wet rip of the skin.

She looked at the blood and gore in Gregory's gaping cavity. She tried to close her nose to the sickening smell of rot wafting up toward her.

Taking a deep breath, she plunged her head into Gregory's innards, slicking her hair with the fluids surrounding them. She brought her head out, feeling the quickly coagulating blood trickle down her back and her face.

She reached her hands into Gregory and pulled out a handful of entrails, draping them around herself, rolling them over her body until she was certain every inch was covered.

By that time, John was nearly upon her.

What next? she thought. *Should I run or should I just let him have me now?*

She stood up from the muck and let out a breath she had been holding in. John turned toward her, charging, and she darted off around the pond.

Twenty-nine

Blood and adrenaline coursed through John.

He could smell the blood of the other—sweet and beautiful and alive—coursing somewhere else. But she wasn't close like she had been before, when he was confined. And she was getting farther away.

His stomach churned. He needed the blood. He needed the meat. He needed the sacrifice.

He would have to hurry.

He needed to find the girl, the prey, and gut her right here under the stars and the cold sliver of the moon.

The tribe demanded it of him. It was all part of the greater cause.

John, with the hybrid life budding within him, needed to make everyone else dead like them, the tribe. Then and only then would he get his chance, his exultation.

And it all had to start here on this small space of land. To continue outward like a disease. Or like a paradise. Ultimately, he had no idea how far it was to spread. His mind, working so slowly beneath the rolling of the need, wasn't so sure any of the rest knew where it was going either.

The thought made John dizzy with excitement.

He imagined something vast and shapeless. Something sprawling out before him. He had no idea what the something was. It might be people. It might be land. This didn't matter to the Johnthing. What mattered was that part of this something-or-the-other, part of this vast future, part, no matter how small, was going to be his. And he was, in a way, the start of this dark future. If he failed now, it was entirely possible the tribe would have no future whatsoever.

The blood. The blood. The blood.

The meat.

A vertigo of craving swirled through him as he breathed deeply, letting that scent surge through his body. The darkly sweet *human* smell blowing like wind across the red hot coals of his need.

But the scent drifted away also.

Slowly. Slowly. Until it was gone completely.

The Johnthing turned in circles, unsure of what was happening. He knew the world, even the night world he thrived in, had shapes and colors—he had felt them the previous nights—and he wondered why the tribe, if it wanted him to succeed so badly, had not also blessed him with the vision of the things he was supposed to kill. The only thing to guide him along was that vibrant red scent splashing through those things. Without that, he was lost. Without that, the night was too dark.

Wait!

Here. He caught a whiff of the scent, of the color—red. He turned toward it, chasing after it, knowing it was not something unobtainable because he had held it before. He had drunk it. But this time he couldn't seem to catch it.

It lingered before drifting away and the Johnthing didn't know if it left on the wind or if it left on the things that carried him across the ground.

Then again, it blossomed in the distance. A fragrant night spice. And again, the Johnthing turned toward it, wanting to pluck the spice. Wanting to hold the scent up to his nose and sniff it until it didn't smell anymore. He wanted to make the need go away.

But it was gone like an illusion and the Johnthing wasn't incredibly sure if it had ever been there in the first place.

Of course there was the other scent. The one that held more meaning for him, for whatever reason, but didn't seem as ripe or as pleasant or as strong as the one that eluded him. The other scent was closer to the stink of death, although not quite. And the Johnthing couldn't figure out why it was supposed to mean something to him. Maybe the other scent, the one he focused on now, was someone that was a little more powerful. Maybe, if he felt some pang of recognition, it was someone the tribe had warned him about. So maybe that was who he should have been after from the beginning. Just because one of the human things *tasted* better didn't necessarily mean it was the better one to kill. Or maybe the other scent's meaning was just some scrap left over from that other part of the Johnthing, the part that existed during the day.

This is what the Johnthing decided to go after.

Tonight, this would have to be his feast.

Thirty

Cassie continued to follow the crazy dream-logic that whispered softly in her head. She was beginning to like that voice. She was beginning to *trust* that voice.

He smells the life, it whispered.

That was the whole reason she'd doused herself in dead blood to begin with. It was a thought that had merely flitted through her head but, for some reason, her mind seized upon it with ferocity.

When she ran, breathing in and out, John chased after her, gaining ground, snarling hungrily.

Stop breathing, the voice whispered.

She wasn't sure how long she would be able to run and hold her breath without passing out but if that was what the voice told her to do, then she was going to do it. She took a deep breath and continued to trudge forward. The combat boots were not the ideal running shoe, she decided.

Over the blood pounding in her oxygen deprived ears, she heard the Johnthing's footsteps falter before coming to a complete stop.

My God, she thought. *The voice was right.*

Then she had another thought. She thought, if the Johnthing

was following her by scent alone, then he must be blind or something. That had to be it. And for the first time since all this craziness began, she felt a sense of power, a feeling she relished, however slight it was.

As more of an experiment than anything, she exhaled at length before sucking in another deep breath. Upon her exhalation, the Johnthing turned sharply in her direction, gaining speed and charging at her.

Once her breath had dissipated, he stopped moving, allowing her to put more ground between them.

In order to broaden this distance as much as possible, she ran back toward the woods until she was sure he was no longer behind her.

Crouching down, obscuring herself as much in the corn as possible, she waited.

Adrenaline and fear kept her pie-eyed until she was sure John had given up. She hadn't been able to see him once she was just a few feet from him but, crouching there, she looked for the smallest movement, listened for the slightest sound. She had already made up her mind that, if she detected any sign of the Johnthing, she would run all the way back to the woods, not stopping until she got there.

She didn't know how long she waited.

Slowly, ever vigilant, she crept back toward the pond. Then she did the thing she had dreaded doing the most.

She approached Gregory and lay down in the grass beside him. She slid an arm between his slick back and the grass beneath it, slowly edging underneath him. Putting her arms between her and Gregory, she felt along his back until she came to one of John's claw marks between his shoulder blades. She stuck her hand in the long gouge and punched it through his body, separating the muscles, using her fingernails to tear through the tough tissue between the ribs, using all of her strength and frustration to grab one of the ribs and snap it downward until she was able to put her arm through to the other side and work it around.

Then she put her face in the gouge and breathed in. She breathed in old blood, felt it trickle into her mouth, but there was air there also. Not a lot. It was kind of like trying to breathe with a quilt pulled up over your face, but it was enough.

It was there Cassie lay, not sleeping, but waiting.

Thirty-one

Gloria Fresk didn't know how long she had been in absolute darkness. It could have been an eternity. It could have been half a day.

She remembered the boom.

And then a something that sounded like the end of the world.

After hearing the sound, she was happy she had not chosen to stand beneath the door to the cellar. Because it collapsed. It did more than collapse. It was actually *driven* into the stone stairway leading into the cellar beneath the force of what Gloria could only imagine was the very house itself.

What else could it have been? Unless a giant meteoroid had come crashing down onto the house. The only thing she could really think about was her predicament. Any reasons she could possibly think of for the house collapsing were beyond her. As far as she knew, earthquakes just did not happen in this part of Ohio. And she didn't think any amount of wind, even a tornado, could knock down the solid stone house.

After the collapse, she had lost consciousness. That was when time stopped meaning anything. She couldn't even begin to guess how long she was out.

When she woke up, she was choking to death. That was probably why she had woken up. Slapped into sudden consciousness, she had stood up, vomiting out the water she had breathed in.

At first, she didn't think anything of it. The ubiquitous water on the cellar floor was one of the reasons she had always avoided coming down here. If it weren't for the water, it would have made a pretty decent place to store stuff.

She splashed through the water, ankle deep, and shouted for help. Panic continued to occlude any explanations she could think of. She couldn't fathom what the hell had happened. She found herself very scared about Gordon and John. Whatever had happened, they were both out there in it. Maybe it was better to be out there than in here, she thought. Hope was not entirely diminished at that point.

It will only be a short while before somebody gets me out of here. What an ugly day this has become. Someone will get me out and then I can hug my husband and my baby and find out what went wrong. I can gain some control of the situation.

It was the last time she would think about having control of anything ever again.

Through the dense blackness, beneath the tight breaths coming from her lungs, she heard the slow trickle of water.

And noticed her small cell was rapidly filling up with it.

Hadn't it just been at her ankles when she stood up?

Now it was up to mid-calf.

She launched herself at the stone wall in front of her that she couldn't see. Crashing into it, she realized how mercilessly ungiving the stones were. She screamed for help. Murderously, frantically, she screamed for helped.

Maybe it wouldn't be so bad, she thought. Maybe it wouldn't be so bad if there was just a single shred, a single scrap of light. In complete blackness, there was nothing for her eyes to adjust to. Everything she did, every movement she made, was based on her prior knowledge of the cellar. This was a knowledge that was not extensive in the least and panic ate away at all knowledge like a rabid carnivore.

Clinging to some of the rocks jutting out from the newly made wall, she tried to climb up even though the roof of the cellar was only a couple of inches above her head.

If she could just find a crack, something to stick her nose through if it got really bad, if the water got too deep...

She had no such luck. So she stood there, clinging frigidly to the wall and waiting. Waiting as the water tickled the backs of her knees. Waiting as the water went up her skirt, ballooning it up around her waist. Waiting as it wrapped her stomach and cupped her breasts. Waiting as it pressed against her chest and delivered its chilly kiss to her neck.

She didn't scream.

She didn't move.

She didn't think.

She stood.

And trembled.

And waited.

Waited for something that never came.

The water never came up past her chin and her rescuer never came, either.

She wondered how long she had stood like that, her head raised just enough to keep the water from covering her mouth. The water, she supposed, actually made it a bit easier, keeping her legs and back from hurting too much. Keeping her at least semi-buoyant.

The only thing she wanted was to get out.

She couldn't think about how she was going to do that. She couldn't think of anyone who could come and save her. She let her thoughts go to God and miracles and air. If she could only taste the air... And wouldn't it be great if the stones were lifted away and it was sunny and everything was just like it had been...

After what happened to Elliot, after a long long period of

thinking the nightmare was never going to end, she found herself thinking it had ended. And maybe, if the nightmare had ended, nothing else bad could happen.

But the nightmare hadn't really ended, had it?

There were still the black dreams, the screaming, the sleeping with the light on. The fear, the constant fear that whoever had taken Elliot would come back for John. It dawned on her that the life she had lead these last twelve years hadn't been much of a life at all. Not life—merely a grim daily reminder of the past. And maybe that kind of life was worse than death. As much as she wanted to embrace every day and thank God for the life that teemed around her, there was still a shadow, a great gray cloud pissing down on her.

Eventually, the water began to recede, but the pace was much slower than when it had risen. It was so slow it took her quite some time to realize it was actually receding. She didn't even want to admit to herself it was receding. She didn't want to allow herself that much hope.

She stood frozen, trying to blank any thought that tried to trespass into her mind. She tried to forget about the constant reminder that her body needed things such as comfort and food.

She couldn't get anything to work. She couldn't get herself to feel Nothing. It felt like bugs crawled on the inside of her skin. Her stomach, filled with nervous acid, churned and roared at her. Her mind, her thinking, began to chase itself in patterns she found reminiscent of sick dreams. Those odd, circular fever dreams, paradoxes where she always felt like she was just a step away from the answer but the answer never came. Indeed, there was no answer, could never be an answer because the rules to these mental games were only logical enough to suck you in and once you were sucked in they became absurd but you were already in and there was no getting out.

No getting out.

There really wasn't any getting out.

What if I never get out? Gloria wondered. *What if there are more booms? What if I run out of oxygen? What if the rocks decide to burst through the ceiling? What if I die of hunger? What if Gordon and John are dead? Would life even be worth living?*

Maybe any of that would be better than dying of starvation like an abandoned animal, left in its cage to rot.

Whatever the outcome would be, she had no say in the matter. She wouldn't have been able to think of any solutions anyway because her mind kept dragging her away through a minefield of depression and fear and panic.

This is, she thought, *the slow warping of my mind.*

And time melted away even further as her body lost whatever circadian rhythm it once had. It dimmed her awareness. She didn't even know if she was still conscious. Did she still stand with her hands and head pressed against the jagged wall? Or was she someplace else? Somewhere outside of her body?

When the rocks were finally pulled away, it took her a few moments to realize someone had done the pulling.

Someone had come to save her!

Her mind started up again, its rust-clogged wheels slowly grinding away. At first she expected to see a stranger. Someone there to tell her her husband and son were dead or in the hospital, comatose in intensive care.

And the face she saw *was* a stranger—kind of.

It wasn't Gordon, that much she was sure of. After the absolute darkness, she couldn't really be sure of *what* her eyes saw.

She cocked her head to the side, studying the face in the dark that didn't really seem so dark compared to the cellar.

Maybe it was John. It didn't really look like John except it kind of did. Maybe, she thought crazily, it's John all grown up. Maybe this has all been some kind of terrible dream. Maybe *I've* been the one in a coma.

She saw arms reach for her and tried to move her own leaden arms toward them, to let John pull her up into a glorious freedom, a new life that would never again be taken for granted.

The arms pulled her up but they weren't aiming to give her any type of new life. They were there to end it.

The hands, large powerful things, landed on her ears and clamped down, wrenching her out of the hole and tossing her onto the warm, dry ground outside.

"John," she tried to say but couldn't open her mouth. Couldn't move her tongue.

When she got a better look at John, she found it impossible to believe this was him at all. This thing hardly looked human. She knew she had to get away and the thing seemed to sense she was virtually defenseless. It let her tremble there on the ground.

She managed to turn over onto her stomach and attempted to struggle to her knees.

Then she felt the claws, like hot curling irons, sink into her back, on the inside of either shoulder blade, and slowly drag their way down, severing anything in their path.

She craned her head up toward the sky, looked at the pale thing trying so hard to be the moon.

Maybe she screamed.

No, she only tried to scream before the blood from her punctured lungs filled the back of her throat and she felt her life leaving with each breath that should have come but wouldn't. She felt the thing feeding behind her, digging its mouth into her back and making sickening wet snarling sounds.

With her mouth mute, her mind screamed red and, before plummeting into the blackness of death, thought, "This is better. This is better."

Thirty-two

John didn't have to see his mother's dead body to know what had happened.

It was well after dawn when he woke up. The sun was already powerful, burning the dew off the dead yellow-brown grass.

He was under the old oak tree. He thought he sensed Cassie when he woke up but maybe it was just some lingering essence trapped in the ground because she wasn't anywhere around.

What he saw first were the remains of the house. Or, rather, the remains of the remains of the house. He stood up and walked over to it, his heart pounding in his chest. The rock pile was depleted, the stones now piled up around the house's foundation. He saw the dark hole leading down to the cellar, a feeling of dread and absence surging through his bones. The same feeling he'd had when he saw his father dead for the first time.

Then he saw other things.

Other things he didn't really want to see. These were things that, a few days ago, he couldn't have fathomed seeing. These sights and feelings, he thought, should have been over with Elliot's disappearance.

Like the trail of blood on the grass, dark and viscous.

Like his car, the trunk folded and punched violently away from the rest of the frame.

Everything Cassie had thought was true.

He was the monster.

The murderer.

He wondered about Cassie.

He wanted to call out for her but he just couldn't do it. He knew his mother was gone, meeting the same violent end as his father, and he realized Cassie was all he had left in the world. Still, he felt emotionless. In just a few brief moments, like a blinding, disheartening flash, he thought he realized the dreadful hopelessness of their situation. That is, if Cassie was still around. Otherwise, it would just be the dreadful hopelessness of *his* situation. By rights, he thought, that's how it should be.

There was no escaping. He had no hopes of escaping and everyone, every*thing* around him seemed to be dead and it was all his fault. If Cassie happened to be dead, he decided he would kill himself. He didn't know how he would do it, but he knew he couldn't go on with the knowledge of his atrocities. If Cassie were still alive, he would seek her opinion. If she actually thought he could help her get out of here, then he would stick around long enough to try and do that.

Slowly, he shuffled over toward the pond (because that was where all the dead people went) and thought about yesterday.

Yesterday now seemed so full of hope compared to this morning. Yesterday, they had had a plan.

Yeah, a plan, but he had also had doubts.

Yesterday, he was only the monster because a beautiful girl he'd never seen before convinced him he was a monster.

Today, there *were* no doubts.

There was nothing except guilt and fear and hopelessness crawling through his intestines like fat acidic slugs. He had never realized what a beautiful thing doubt actually was.

He reached the field and walked up the slight slope toward the pond.

Despite his depression, he nearly smiled when he saw Cassie flopping around in the pond. If he had been with her, he never would have let her get in there, remembering the way it had twisted down into what he now thought could have only been hell.

Any smiles or feelings of goodness he had were quickly wiped away when he saw the third corpse lying out by the pond.

And that was it. It was one thing to think about it. It was another to see it lying starkly before him.

He didn't know what to do. A surge of anger blossomed up from his soul and he took off running toward the woods. Anything to get away from the reality of his nocturnal life. A life that almost had to be some inner reflection of himself.

So he turned his back on the dead things. Turned his back on the beautiful naked girl in the pond and ran.

His legs and lungs burned. His hair was hot on his head. Sweat covered his skin as he hit the big eastern field, all that corn (*more death*) crunching beneath his feet.

He ran until he hit a rock and went flying down into the cracked earth, as hard as concrete.

And there he lay, thinking about everything and nothing and wishing he had a gun to put in his mouth or some pills to put in his stomach.

There he cried, making no attempt to hold it in. He rolled over, turned his back to the sun and cried into his arm, smelling the dead dog shit earth beneath him.

Thirty-three

Cassie pulled herself from the stinkwater of the pond feeling refreshed and clean. She had removed one of John's dad's socks to use as a washcloth, wanting something to scour the disgusting gore caked to her skin. Once out, she didn't see any sign of John so she decided to leave her clothes off a little bit longer. They were currently soaking in the pond also. She knew they would still stink when she put them on.

When she had woken up that morning, she saw another body lying on the other side of John's dad. It was a very attractive, blond, middle-aged woman Cassie figured had to be John's mom. Cassie had crouched down on her knees and said a short prayer over the body.

In a way, she felt partially responsible for the woman's death. What if she could have done something to fend John off? Or found some way to distract him until dawn?

No, she told herself. She hadn't even thought he would be able to rip his way out of the trunk, let alone clear away the whole goddamned house.

She had done her best to survive and she didn't think anybody else would have done any differently. Under the circumstances, she didn't think there was anything she *could* have done differently.

She drifted away from the pond. After bathing, she noticed the smell surrounding it was atrocious… all those dead things. She let the sun dry the water on her body and wondered about what she and John were going to do that evening. In a way, they had kind of run out of possibilities.

She wasn't so certain that covering herself in the smell of the dead would work again tonight. Last night, John had apparently just moved onto his mother. But she didn't know if he would give up so easily tonight with nothing to fall back on.

Let's not think about that now, she told herself.

Once the sun had dried her down to the scalp, she went back to the pond, put her dripping wet clothes back on and went in the direction of the house, in search of John and food.

Thirty-four

John stayed out in the field all morning, first lying and then sitting. He really hadn't considered moving until he heard Cassie calling for him. Even then he thought he should just get up and charge into that force field or whatever the hell it was and let it drive him down into death. Even when she yelled, "I found food," he didn't want to get up and go. Of course, he didn't *need* to get up and go. He had been eating fine the entire time. Call it cannibal cuisine.

A belly full of Mom, he thought, wishing that thought hadn't popped into his head.

The best thing he could do, he figured, was to talk this over with Cassie. Get her opinion. Maybe she had some different thoughts than he did. Some better thoughts.

He stood up and dusted off his ass.

Thirty-five

When he got up by the house, John saw Cassie sitting under the oak tree, eating an orange and reading *Vampires in Devil Town*. She hadn't heard him and when she finally noticed him her reaction was that of a person caught masturbating. She had been savoring the orange, relishing it, feeling its cool, biting juices slide down her throat.

He approached her. She dropped her eyes and mumbled, "I'm sorry."

"It's okay," he said. "I know what happened. I should be sorry for doubting you. Maybe if I hadn't doubted you so much, we could have found some other way."

"No, I wasn't a hundred percent sure myself."

"What are we gonna do about tonight?"

"I was kind of hoping *you* had some plans."

"No. I'm fresh out." He tried to force a smile.

"We'll think of something."

"If not, I know what I have to do."

"Let's not think about that."

"You know what I have to do too."

"Let's not think about it."

"You found the refrigerator?"

"Yeah. It was pretty smashed up. But there's some things we can eat in there. Hungry?"

"No." He looked guiltily at his feet. "And you found my book."

"It was under a rock near the refrigerator. It's funny. I was actually reading this book. Had to... leave it in my bag when the storm hit."

"We're probably like the only two people on the planet to read that book."

"Maybe it means we're soul mates."

John tried to force a laugh but the sad sarcasm of the comment struck him as too true. He hung his head to keep from crying.

"You know," she said. "It has to get better. It's like Murphy's Law or something, isn't it? How does that Doors song go, 'I've been down so long it looks like up to me?' Or something like that."

"You like the Doors?" John asked, realizing they hadn't talked about themselves very much.

"Well, not really. I just had this friend that was really into them. She had posters of Jim Morrison all over her room. I think she was hoping he would like come back from the dead or something. She made me quite sick of the Doors."

"Hmmm," John said, embarrassingly thinking about the "American Poet" poster he had hanging in his room until the end of high school.

They talked like that for quite a while, trying to make something out of nothing, realizing they had very few things in common. She talked about her friends at St. Agnes and some of her friends from town. Those were the names he recognized. They were far from the jock and cheerleading assholes but they were still a group that would never have had anything to do with John. They were, he guessed, from the art and slacker crowd—as much of one as Lynchville had, anyway. In Lynchville, it seemed you either modeled yourself after your parents, pro athletes, or MTV. John had often thought about Cassie's people as being just about like everybody else, except they looked different. They still had the endless thirst to belong.

John, because he had no friends to talk about, did most of the listening, trying not to be too judgmental. It also made him realize, with his parents gone, how very much alone he actually was. He guessed he wouldn't be able to continue driving everyone away with his unrelenting bitterness.

Finally, after slaking their thirsts and eating some more fruit from the demolished refrigerator, they started talking about their plans for that evening.

"This time I guess we try one of the other cars," Cassie said. "I imagine they both have the automatic trunk thingies."

"Yeah," John confirmed.

"Okay. So we'll break out the window with a rock. When you get in the trunk—we'll have to do this earlier than last night—I'll pile some rocks on there."

"Why don't you just kill me?"

She laughed, as though it had never even entered her mind. "I couldn't do that."

"I'm serious. You know you're next, right?"

"Not if I can help it."

"I don't even want it to be an issue. If not you, then somebody else."

"I'm beginning to wonder if there *is* anybody else."

"Yeah, me too." He paused. "I mean, how much longer can we go on like this?"

"Let's bust out that window."

He picked up a large stone that was still small enough to throw with some momentum.

"Just promise me," he said. "That if you're in any danger and you can, you know, get rid of me, you won't hesitate. I know what has to be done. I don't think I could live with myself if I kill anybody else. I'm not sure I can live with myself now."

They meandered over to his father's green Taurus. He hoisted the rock toward the driver's side window of the car. The rock hit it and bounced off, crashing into the gravel of the driveway.

"We'll cross that bridge if we come to it," Cassie said.

"What bridge?"

"The killing-John bridge."

He bent to pick up the rock.

"Let me try that," she said. "It looks like fun."

He handed her the rock. She raised it up and down in her hands, getting a feel for its heft. Then she brought it up above her head and sent it arcing toward the window. It smashed the glass easily and landed in the front seat. "Ah-hah," she said. "Girl power rules again."

"Lucky shot."

"Lucky my ass. Face it boy, I'm stronger than you."

"I wouldn't doubt that."

"You calling me butch," she faked offense.

"No, far from it. Quite the opposite. I'd probably consider myself girly before I considered you manly. You're, uh..." He hesitated. "Everything a girl should be."

"Well, thank you, Mr. John."

"Much obliged."

"We gonna open the door or what?"

"That would be the next logical step, wouldn't it?"

She stuck her head in the car, the intense heat swarming her. There was something else she noticed as she pulled the door handle from the inside. It was a familiar scent, magnified to fill up the closed car in the searing heat. She took a deep breath.

"This is your dad's car, right?"

"Yeah."

"Your old man smoke pot?"

He didn't really know. He'd never thought about it. He didn't think parents did that but, then again, his dad had never sat him down and had a big drug talk, either. Even after the Jim Morrison poster.

"I don't know," he said.

"You said he, what, worked for the nature reserve?"

"Yeah."

"Well, John," she reached under the passenger seat and came up with a baggie. "I think your old man was a pothead."

"Bravo," he said sarcastically.

"No. That's good. I think we just found our entertainment for the afternoon." She held up the bag. "Jesus, that's a lot of pot."

Then she noticed the look on John's face. "Oh God, don't tell me you haven't smoked pot."

"Well, not exactly. I've just, uh, never had the chance, I guess."

"So you'll start now. It's okay. There's still time for you yet."

She pulled the cardboard sleeve of Job papers out of the baggie and went about rolling a thin joint. He didn't know what it was but he found something incredibly sexy about this act. Once rolled, she reached back into the car and felt around on the floor until she came up with a green Bic.

"You first," she said, handing it over to John. "It's bad luck to take the first toke from the one you rolled."

He inspected the joint, wondering which end he should stick in his mouth.

"It doesn't matter," she said.

He stuck the joint in his mouth and touched the lighter to it like he was lighting a cigarette, which was something else he'd never done. It merely burnt the twist of paper at the end away and he inhaled strange tasting air.

She took the lighter and held it up. "Here, try again," she said.

He took a deep drag as she held the lighter to the end. Smoke scorched down his throat and exploded in his lungs. He coughed it all back out, his eyes watering.

"Okay," she said. "Don't suck so hard."

This time he took a smaller hit, kept it held into his lungs like he'd seen people do in movies. Exhaling, he found the taste rather pleasant.

She pressed the joint between her lips and inhaled, bringing it away and holding it delicately between her thumb and index finger.

"My God, that's nice," she said, handing the joint back to John. "Now we just need some cool music and..." She headed over to the oak tree. "Some fucking shade. Sorry, John, looks like you'll have to sing."

He took his drag and handed it back. "I don't think anybody'd want to hear that."

"Oh come on."

"This stuff couldn't make me high enough to sing. Not a chance in hell."

"Look around you, John." She laughed. "We're *in* hell."

"Don't remind me," he said.

"We could read some of that book out loud."

This made them both laugh hysterically.

They sat down under the tree and passed the joint. He called it quits after the fourth toke. It felt like his lungs were bleeding. She took one more hit and roached it against the tree.

Thirty-six

They lay with their heads resting against the tree, oddly angled away from each other. John, his hands clasped over his stomach and ankles crossed, couldn't help but look over at Cassie. Her arms rested on the ground, palms facing up in a way he found somewhat yogic. Her right leg was flat on the ground, her left knee drawn up, her skirt gathered just below her crotch. Glassy-eyed, she stared off into the distance.

He didn't really know what he was feeling. He guessed it was probably the pot, but it was new and exciting. Somehow, his worry melted away. His eyes felt dry but it was okay because he didn't think he needed to blink. Everything became more sensual. The heat on his skin sank in, all the way down to the bone. Everything seemed clearer but in an odd way. It was like he didn't notice the definition of things but he realized how they contrasted—the burnt, amber brown field in front of him extending upward, green trees (outside the zone) wavering in a breeze that wasn't around him. Beyond that, and overtop of them, the blueness of the sky.

He didn't know how long it was before one of them finally spoke. He didn't care.

"I really am sorry that all this has happened to you," she said.

"It's happened to you, too."

"No. Well, I know. But what I meant was… about your parents. When we get out of here, I still have a family to go back home to, hopefully."

"Maybe it just hasn't really hit me yet. You know, none of this seems real. I just keep telling myself that they're gone and there's nothing I can do to get them back. I mean, they were going to die sometime or the other, right?"

"That's one way of looking at it."

"It's like mourning seems like it's done more for the living than the dead, don't you think?"

"But it's natural to cry."

"Oh, I did plenty of that this morning, believe me. What hurts most is knowing I had something to do with it. Hell, I *did* it…"

"No, John, I've seen this thing. It's not you."

"Then what is it? Have you stopped to think about that? Just what the fuck is it?"

"I don't know. There's no telling. I'm like you, this whole thing doesn't even feel real to me. Everything's been really fucked up since that goddamn storm. But that… *thing*… you should just stop right now from thinking that it's you. Unless you're a lot more fucked up than I think you are. Something… I don't know. It's almost like something's *using* you."

"That's what it feels like. I don't remember any of it and then I wake up the next morning feeling like I should be going to bed I'm so fucking tired."

"So maybe something *is* using you. Have you really stopped to think about why any of this is happening?"

She put her knee down, tucked her skirt in between her legs and rolled over on her side, facing him, her head resting on her right hand.

"I haven't had time to think about it a whole lot and, I guess when I have had time, I've been thinking of ways to get out—not thinking about what happened."

"Yeah, but I mean, if you had to guess what was going on around us, what would you say it was?"

"It's pretty farfetched."

"Go ahead. I think this whole scenario's been pretty farfetched, myself."

"You'll probably think I'm nuts."

"Maybe I already do."

"Okay, well, when you ask me how I can react so calmly to my parents' death, it's because I've been through it all before. I don't mean my parents but, when I was seven, my brother was killed."

"I'm so sorry."

"The worst thing is that nobody really knows how he was killed. He's really just been missing all these years."

Silence wrapped them as Cassie lay there, not knowing what to say, and John tried to collect his thoughts.

"But, if I think about it, I think all of this is somehow connected."

"This is connected with your brother's disappearance?"

"Okay..." he sat up, facing her completely, his legs crisscrossed. "I think something *is* inside of me. If it's human, I think it has some type of power or something. I think it's trying to reach out— to destroy as many people as possible so it can clear the way for something else, something bigger."

"Now, tell me *why* you think that."

"Have you ever heard of the Devils?"

Thirty-seven

Cassie, possibly forgetting the gravity of the situation, kind of chortled. "Well, yeah, everyone around here's heard of the Devils."

"Well," John said. "I don't really think they're just a myth."

"I think, at this point, I would almost believe you." She paused and looked at the butchered copy of *Vampires in Devil Town* on the ground. "You know..."

"I *do* know," John said. "I read it four times and didn't make the connection until just a second before the storm."

"Too weird."

"I think the Devils had something to do with Elliot's disappearance and I think they have something to do with this."

So John told her about what happened when he was seven years old:

It was winter. December 18th, to be exact. It had been a perfectly normal day. John and Elliot had gone off to school and rode the bus back home. Elliot was fourteen, so he was in charge of John until their parents came back from work. He was good at it, too. John had often thought that, if some men were born fathers, then Elliot would be one of those men. He was never harsh. He never hit John. He always explained to John why what he was doing might not be such a good idea.

When they came home that day, Elliot made them peanut butter sandwiches and turned the afternoon cartoons on. John ate his peanut butter sandwich and drank his Pepsi and watched cartoons while Elliot ate his own sandwich and read. John couldn't stress enough how completely routine this was and now he wondered how he could have ever taken something so routine for granted. Sure, there were some days when he thought it was boring. There were other days when he grumbled at Elliot because he wanted Elliot to play with him. If he ever would have known those routine days could possibly come to an end then he would have cherished every second of them.

As the afternoon grew into evening, the only abnormal thing to insert itself was the storm.

On that day that seemed so long ago, it had been a snowstorm and John regarded it, much as he did thunderstorms, with his childish awe of how much snow it could produce.

His mother and father came home before the snow got too deep. They were actually home a little earlier than usual. Gloria went about preparing a simple but homemade dinner, just like she did every night, while Gordon sat in front of the television and watched the news.

The snow continued to fall.

John didn't bother with the tiny amount of homework he had because, by the time dinner was ready, all Lynchville schools were closed for the next day. He was excited. It meant he would probably be able to stay up a little bit later than usual tonight and would get to sleep in tomorrow. And tomorrow was Friday and that made it seem like a vacation although with the amount of snow it looked like they were going to get, he almost wished it was a Wednesday so the vacation would be even longer.

Elliot had disappeared upstairs to his bedroom when his parents came home. That wasn't unusual. He spent most of his time up there these days, reading, watching the TV in his room, or talking on the phone. Sometimes John went in there and sat in on him while he did these things (except talking on the phone—Elliot always shooed him away when he was on the phone) mostly because he just enjoyed being around his big brother.

The only interesting thing John could think of that happened occurred at dinnertime.

Elliot had come down to eat after Gloria had called up to him that dinner was ready. He came downstairs somewhat belatedly and, rather than eating, simply sat in his chair and stared at the food. He continued to stare until everyone else at the table was staring at him.

"Is something the matter?" Gloria asked.

"I'm just... I'm just not feeling very well," Elliot said. "I think I might just go back upstairs."

And that whole part was the thing John remembered very well. He remembered thinking about how awful it was Elliot wasn't feeling well because tomorrow was a snow day and it would really suck to be sick on a snow day. It was only kind of good to be sick when you could get out of school and you couldn't get out of school if there wasn't any. That would be like getting sick on the weekend.

And John remembered the pall that settled over the table after Elliot stood up and shuffled off into the living room to go back upstairs; how everyone else just kind of sat around awkwardly before their own food.

And John remembered, so very clearly, the sparse dialogue between mother and son:

Is something the matter?

I'm just... I'm just not feeling very well.

One of the reasons he thought he remembered it so vividly was because Elliot had said he wasn't feeling "well" instead of "good." He thought Elliot was really smart and that was always one of the reasons John liked to be around him. Everyone else he knew would have said "good" except for maybe his English teacher. But Elliot had said that he just... just wasn't feeling very well. And John really didn't think anything about it until he went to bed that night. Then he remembered praying just like he did every night and prayed Elliot would feel better in the morning so he could play with him on their snow day.

He went to sleep, just like he always did, and when he woke up, the nightmare began.

He awoke cloaked in fear. He was covered in sweat and his heart pounded. Something had happened to Elliot. He knew this. He got out of bed. The house was quiet and dark. The door to his parents' bedroom was closed but Elliot's was open. That was a little strange. Normally, John was the only one who slept with his door open.

He stood at the threshold of his brother's room, staring into the darkness, trying to figure out if he could make out Elliot's shape in his bed. But it was too dark. The only light afforded was the weak purple glow filtering in through the windows.

"Elliot," John whispered.

The black seconds dripped tar slow in the quiet house.

"Elliot," he whispered again.

And again, there was nothing.

He stood there, nearly frozen. If Elliot was sick and sleeping and John was just acting like a crazy scared kid, then he didn't want to bother him. But what if something *had* happened to Elliot. Deep down, John felt like something most definitely bad had happened to Elliot. And he didn't think anything good could happen this late at night. Continuing to stand, he tried to figure out if he could actually hear Elliot breathing or if it was just the wind or the furnace. Finally, he broke his paralysis and approached the bed.

As he drew closer, his fear subsided somewhat because he was almost certain he could see Elliot lying in bed beneath the covers. If he could just put his hands on Elliot and know he was there and that he was breathing then everything would be okay and then he could go climb back in his warm bed and look forward to the snow day tomorrow.

He reached his hand toward the lump of covers, half-expecting to feel Elliot's solidity beneath them.

But he didn't. His hand merely pressed the covers, mashing them down onto the bed.

It was nearly impossible to describe what happened next. Something inside of John broke. He could feel it. He almost thought he could hear it. A part of him expanded, yawning out into some unknown void or abyss.

He no longer knew if he should do what he knew he was *supposed* to or if he should do what he knew he *had* to.

What he ought to have done, he knew, was go wake up his parents. But that something inside of him… That new something that had just poked out its head told him that telling his parents would only slow things up, that if he wanted to find Elliot, he would have to go now. And it was telling him exactly where he needed to go.

At that point, he just kind of stopped thinking. He moved as though hypnotized. He went downstairs and through the living room and through the kitchen, moving toward something he could not fathom. He moved through the enclosed back porch and out into the cold and the snow, barefoot, totally unconscious of the wind and unimpeded by the snow rising to his knees.

Outside, the moon was bright and full and the blanket of fresh, unbroken snow made everything seem even brighter. He could see almost as well as he could during the daytime except the sky was black and star-filled.

Was that Elliot shuffling along in the distance in front of him?

He thought maybe it was. He certainly hoped it was. And why couldn't John call out to him? Why couldn't he yell out to him and tell him to hold up? *Hey, Elliot! You're sick, come back inside!* But none of the words would come.

Maybe it didn't matter anyway because he couldn't be sure if that was Elliot up there or not. One minute he thought he saw somebody and the next minute there wasn't anything at all.

And, if it was Elliot, or anybody at all really, why weren't there some kind of footprints in the snow?

People walking through the snow left footprints, didn't they?

That other part of John, the new part, the part that had just splintered away from the old John, told him that, maybe, whatever it was he followed through the snow was not a person at all.

He followed anyway. He followed because he had to. So off he went across the expansive backyard and the barren field and into the woods. The entire time, he felt nothing, not even the passage of time. His insides felt frozen while his physical body, the part that *should* have been frozen, moved him along rapidly.

Before he knew it, he was in the woods. The snow wasn't nearly as deep here and it felt so warm.

Along the narrow trails he went, past trees and down toward the thick of the woods, chasing Elliot, chasing some feeling it would take him the rest of his life to try and figure out.

Then, when it was time to stop, he stopped.

And stared.

It took him a minute to realize what it was he saw.

And then he realized the reason everything looked so odd was because he was seeing two things at once. It was like he was standing there and staring at two completely different places that were kind of overlapping.

Immediately in front of him he saw a boy, or a man, he couldn't be completely sure which. At first, he thought it was Elliot but then he realized the boy was not Elliot—he was one of the people who had taken Elliot. But, the confusing thing was the way the boy just stood there, staring at him. His black eyes gleamed in the darkness. There was a look of guilt or concern or something John didn't necessarily associate with bad things in those eyes.

Behind the boy was some kind of scene John knew could not be here in these woods. Because John and Elliot had been all over these woods in the summertime and never had they seen anything like this. The other strange thing about this other scene John looked upon was that it was daylight. A blue cloudless sky hovered overhead. Below the sky were the hills, green with summer and humming with life. He could feel the hum of myriad insects and plants in a constant state of slow growth. And there, in the middle of the hills was a huge, sad-looking house. He looked at the house and felt a sense of nostalgia and familiarity, knowing he had never seen the house before.

And then everything started to spin.

He heard Elliot crying for help, the scream of the cold winter wind, the susurrating rhythm of the insects, all blazing through his head with ferocity while he felt himself being sucked back and back and back and when he woke up the next day it was to the sounds of his parents talking to the police downstairs.

He had things to tell them. He knew he had things to tell them. Big important things like where Elliot was and a description of the boy who might have taken him or, if *he* hadn't taken him, then he at least knew who had.

But John couldn't remember what any of that big important stuff was and, by the time he reached the kitchen he couldn't even think of why he had hurried down there. It was like nothing had happened at all.

Thirty-eight

"Wow," Cassie said. "I don't think I've heard you say that much since we've been around each other. So you've never told anybody about this?"

"I had totally blocked out everything until all of this shit with the storm. Hell, now I still can't even be sure it really happened or if I'm just remembering it that way."

"But you think all of this has something to do with your brother?"

"Kind of. I'm thinking it all has something to do with the Devils and I think *they* have something to do with Elliot's disappearance."

"And, you said before, you think *they've* taken some kind of control over you?"

"Yeah. I'm pretty sure. They or somebody like them."

"Why do you say that?"

"When I was there, the night that Elliot disappeared, I saw that kid just standing there and I don't know, I just don't see how someone like him could be capable of all of this. I'm kind of thinking that, if the Devils are real, then maybe they're just like everybody else. You know, you take any group of people and you're going to have good people and bad people."

"I think I understand. So who do you think took Elliot? Was it the good people or the bad people?"

"I just… Jesus, I really don't know. I guess we might figure it out eventually, huh?"

They sat in silence for a few seconds, staring up at the unwavering blue sky as if some faint glimmer of hope was hidden up there. He nervously played with a blade of dead grass. He had debated with himself about telling her about his more recent foray into the woods. He knew, if he told her about that, he would have to tell her everything about it and some parts were kind of embarrassing.

"That's not, uh, all of the story, either," he said, clearing his throat and preparing to talk again.

So, again, he told her everything. About how, for some reason, he had wanted to stay out in the storm. He told her about the pond and every little detail about the strange dream he'd had. It really wasn't until he told her about it that he realized how eerily similar it had been to what happened to him twelve years ago. And it really wasn't until telling her about it he realized it probably wasn't a dream at all. It also dawned on him that, of course, those people had put something inside of him. He knew, in the human world, it wasn't really possible but these people seemed to operate under some kind of weird nightmare biology, the understanding of which, he knew, was well outside his grasp.

Cassie made a great listener. She didn't say anything. There were not any interruptions. She didn't nod her head or do any of those fake things people who aren't listening do to make people think they *are* listening. She just lay there, on her side, looking up at him with those sparkly, unreal green eyes and never taking them off him.

Cassie struck John as a sincere person. At first, when he had begun telling her the whole crazy story, he had half-expected her to laugh in his face. But as he continued on with the second part he watched her look grow more and more serious. By the end, he thought she now maybe realized just how involved in his story she really was. Since she couldn't leave, she was just as much a part of this as he was.

"'Only the dead can leave,'" she said. "Wonder what the hell that's supposed to mean."

"I don't know. There's so much about all of this shit that I just don't understand. I don't ever hardly leave the house. I'm terrified of the fact I don't even understand humans. How am I possibly supposed to understand any of this shit?"

She stared down into the grass, running her fingers along it. He thought it looked like she was pretending there was actual grass there, as opposed to the dried and shriveled grass that actually covered the ground.

She reached over and playfully patted him on the knee. She tried to smile but the smile kind of faltered and John didn't like the look of that.

"Well, I hate to be a downer but I think I have some more shit to throw at you."

"What is it?"

"I don't know. I'll have to tell you about it. It's possible that it could be a good thing but I want to get your opinion on it. Stuff has been happening to me too. And I think it just might go right along with everything you've been telling me about."

"Well, what is it?"

"Elliot."

Thirty-nine

She took a deep breath and, even though she was obviously much better at speaking than John, she still looked down at the ground, as if searching it for the words to her story.

"I had a dream too. I mean, there are dreams and then there are things that border closely on something more like a different reality. A vision, maybe? Or maybe it really happened. I don't know. In dreams, there's always something that doesn't make sense or some details you can't remember. Like when you talk to somebody and you know it's like one of your friends but, in the *dream*, it looks like a teacher or something. But my dream is like yours, I remember everything about it."

"Are you going to tell me?"

"Yeah, but I need to tell you some other things too. So the dream makes sense. I need to tell you what happened to me during the storm."

"Okay."

And she told him about Gregory.

She told him about how afraid she was. About how she felt like she no longer had any control of her actions whatsoever and, above all, about how she didn't feel as if she really had a choice to be here or not. It was like something else had chosen her fate for her. And how she couldn't help but think this is exactly where she belonged. She really didn't know how to feel about any of that. It almost felt like she had been raped by Gregory, even though she hadn't been. There was maybe even the tiniest part of her that thought, if she had just given Gregory what he wanted back in the car at the dam, then none of this would be happening to her right now. Meanwhile, there was another part of her that knew, if they actually came through this nightmare alive, all of her actions were the right ones.

John's eyes looked hurt and she thought he was nearly shaking with anger.

"I guess one of my points is, whatever these people we're dealing with are, there seems to be something about them that feeds off of our hopes and fears. Like the dream or vision or whatever I had couldn't have happened if I wasn't feeling like a lost and scared little girl."

Then she told him about *her* dream.

"The funny thing about it," she said. "Is that I don't even remember going to sleep last night. I mean, I think I drifted off for a little bit this morning but the sun was already coming up. I think I was way too scared to fall asleep while it was actually dark.

"Anyway, I guess I *must* have dozed off or something because your brother woke me up. I knew it was your brother. I might have even known his name was Elliot before you told me. He woke me up and told me to follow him. I didn't question it or anything, you know, because it was a dream and it doesn't seem like you can ever really question a dream. So I got up and followed him and it was like before dawn, you know. Like when everything is just kind of blue and gray and maybe pink but you can't see the sun yet. And he was walking out toward the field there..." She gestured toward the east field. "And I had this really strange thought like he was gonna lead me straight into the dawn and I was thinking about how spectacular it would be and as I followed him I kept watching him

and I noticed he seemed kind of like part of the sky. He was…
well, he wasn't *blue* but this bluish glow surrounded him or
something and when he walked it almost looked like he wasn't
moving at all. Then I had this other thought that I really wished
you could be there. I knew it was just a dream but I still wanted
you to see him, you know… like see your brother come back as
just some type of beautiful angel. Because that was really how I
thought of him. He seemed so insubstantial that he almost had to
be like pure energy or something. And I knew that, whatever it was
he was leading me toward couldn't be anything bad. I almost had
goosebumps the entire time you were talking about him going
missing because I think a part of me felt that whole story in a
matter of seconds.

"So I followed him and wondered where he was going because I
didn't think I'd be able to follow him I felt so heavy and sore, like
the ground was trying to pull me down in it or something but I just
kept going and hoping we got there soon. Also, as we kept walking
along it was like your brother was almost disappearing. He was
getting thinner so that I could see the woods right through him and
I was almost afraid I would lose him completely if I didn't hurry
the fuck up so I started running, or trying to run. There was kind
of a mist or something too and it almost made it worth running, to
feel that moisture on my face and arms.

"That field was a lot farther away than it looked standing back
at the meadow but I managed to reach it. When I got there, I didn't
see any signs at all of your brother. I looked around and wanted to
call for him but I didn't know what to yell. I didn't think it was
right to just yell 'Hey, you.' So I went deeper into the woods and I
realized they weren't all dead. If anything, they were the opposite.

"Everything seemed almost too alive. The trees and bushes and
moss and stuff all looked more green than I've ever seen them at
the reserve. So I just kept going in because I thought this would
probably be a better place to sleep than back in that ugly field that
smells like dead things and I could hear the rain coming down on

the trees and draining down into the woods. And it wasn't cold rain either. It was as warm as bath water.

"All I could think about was how tired and sore I was and about how I'd never get out of this whole fucking miserable situation and then I saw Elliot again. At first I wanted to run because of all the shit that's been happening. I kind of freaked out, I guess. But when I saw the look in his eyes I knew he wasn't there to hurt me.

"I laid down on the ground and let the raindrops hit me in the eyes and felt like I was just melting right into the ground. It was the first time since before the storm I've felt anything even remotely resembling comfort. Elliot got down on his knees beside me and moved his hands all over me and it was like he was trying to take away the pain. It was like he removed all the fear and all the shit with Gregory and everything. It made me feel lighter or, fuck, I don't know, *unburdened* or something.

"When he was finished I had this tingly feeling all over my body and I knew that was the best feeling I'd ever felt before in my life and I sat their sinking into this dream and just thinking about how beautiful it was and how I never wanted to wake up and… Jesus, I'm still really high. What kind of shit does your dad smoke anyway?" Cassie laughed nervously through the tears streaming down her cheeks.

"So my brother disappears and becomes a spiritual masseuse."

Cassie kept laughing. It made John feel a little better.

Forty

"Is that all of it?" John asked.

"Yeah. The next thing I remember was laying there in the field."

"So we need to try and put these things together."

"I think that would be a good idea."

"We obviously shouldn't be too rational about this."

"Be inventive or die."

"Is this avant-garde survival?"

"I guess so."

They both sat there, staring at the ground, staring at the panoramic prison surrounding them.

John spoke. "Okay. So we have to figure out if we want to look at the dreams as things that don't physically exist or if we want to view the dreams as reality."

"Or, maybe the dreams were like signals. Maybe they were there to illuminate us."

"That would be kind of the middle ground, wouldn't it? And there's the book..."

"The vampire book?"

"I think we have to consider it."

"That seems almost crazy."

"What about this doesn't seem crazy?"

"True... but..."

"I'm not saying it's nonfiction or anything but, in *that* book there's a book called *The Leaves of Six* and a person has to read that before graduating into an upper level Devil. Maybe here, this is that book."

Cassie kind of wrinkled her nose. "I don't know. Maybe I need to finish reading it."

"Okay. Maybe we'll come back to it. So what do the dreams tell us?"

"Well, there's clearly a light and dark thing happening. In yours, there is the group of thirteen, traditionally a bad luck number. Witches' covens typically have thirteen members but that doesn't necessarily mean anything."

"Right."

"Yours were predominantly male, headed by a female. My dream just had Elliot. Your guys were obviously the evil ones. The Devils. Mine had me and a good person doing good things."

"But, based on the dream I had as a child, the Devils may not be all bad. Like, Elliot could be a Devil too."

"Okay. So the Devils put something inside of you. They're using you for something. What could they be using you for?"

"I'm not sure. You know, in high school, I took a class in anthropology and the teacher said the reason for all war came down to resources. By resources he meant like land and labor and virtually everything but I don't think the concept of war is that different than what we're facing. They're using me. I'm a resource. And they have clearly staked out a certain area of land and maybe they have some use for other humans also. Or maybe they're trying to do away with humans altogether."

"That all sounds perfectly legitimate. So you, my friend, are basically the link between them and us."

"Yeah, I'm pretty well aware of that."

"I could just take you out. Sever that link." She drew a finger across her throat and chuckled.

"I've thought of that. Believe me."

"Then our job, basically, is to stop them."

"But there's so much we don't understand."

"That's the beauty of the world, John. You don't understand any of it. I think maybe you just need to get out a little bit more. If you just stay inside, always studying, always trying to understand, then you'll just paralyze yourself."

He thought those were probably the most honest words that had ever been spoken to him.

"You're right," he said. "I don't really think we have much time to waste. It's only been like three days and my entire world has been destroyed."

"So we're agreed that what we need to do is stop them."

"Yes."

"Now we just need some kind of plan."

"Right. Maybe a different plan than what we've been using."

"So far we've been on the defensive."

"And we're supposed to become offensive."

"Exactly."

"That's kind of hard to do if we don't know what it is we're supposed to be... offending. And we can only work during the daylight, which doesn't exactly seem to be abundant."

"No. *You* can only work in the daylight. I can still work at night provided you are all safe and secure."

"Too bad this couldn't have happened around a prison."

"And I'm afraid today might almost be shot. See what the drugs'll do to you, John? They turn you into a shiftless layabout."

"A shiftless layabout with ideas, though, goddammit."

"Okay, any ideas as far as a plan goes?"

"Well, I think it's fairly obvious the storm had something to do with this. I mean, the last time it happened, when they took Elliot, there was a storm, too. Only, that time, it was a snowstorm."

"Yeah, I was thinking that too."

"Life was so good before the storm."

"You can't think that way."

"I know."

"So, maybe if this last storm did this, maybe the next one can somehow undo it."

"But how do we know when it's coming?"

"Well, we certainly won't have more than a few hours notice, if that. There isn't exactly a wealth of weather forecasters out here. But, look at it this way—it's June in Ohio. Normally, you can count on a good thunderstorm a week. Or at least a day of rain. So it should be any day now."

"We should probably have our plan ready as soon as possible. So we'll know what the hell we're doing. And we can't rely totally on the idea that a storm would undo it. I mean, we don't really have anything to prove that."

"You're right. But I really do think the storms have a lot to do with it. I think that it's kind of like what you were saying about all the energy. I think it provides like a vortex or a cover or something like that."

"Jesus, I feel like we've fallen into a really bad science fiction movie. We're talking nonsense."

"John, we've experienced nothing *but* nonsense the past few days."

"This is true. Which brings me back to the book."

Cassie rolled her eyes. "Okay. Let's hear your book theory."

"Okay. This is mostly intuition and if I'm wrong and we both die or if just *you* die horribly and painfully, you have to promise not to hold it against me."

"I think that was sarcasm but, if you want an answer then, yes, I promise not to hold it against you."

"Okay. So in the book there's a house that kind of holds the head Devils. They can't leave. And beneath the house is something called the Low Church. Stay with me. And in the church is something called the Dark Fire. Beyond that is the world of the

Devils. It's where some of them are trapped. I'm just saying this because if we really are going on the offensive, then we should know where to find them."

"And this church is... where?"

"I was getting to that. I think it's beneath the pond."

"Great. So we'll just get some scuba gear and go spelunking or whatever."

"I think spelunking is caves but, that's okay, you go to private school. Anyway, I think if another storm does come back, they'll want to get out and the same thing will happen."

"I wish I could believe you."

"I wish I could be sure of this myself. Like I said, it's just a feeling. Sometimes I learn more from what's not in a book than what's in it. I almost feel like, in a way, we're the boy and the girl in the book. It's almost like if you filled in everything that wasn't said about them, it could be us."

"Did you know Mark David Chapman shot John Lennon so more people would know about *Catcher in the Rye*? Don't be Mark David Chapman."

"You have to admit there are more than a few similarities."

"Between what?"

"The Devils. Lynchville. The woman."

"Okay. I will entertain the thought."

They fell into silence again, knowing sunset wasn't that far off.

"Kind of hungry," John said, just to say something. He wasn't really hungry at all.

"Me, too."

They stood up, full of stiff lethargy, and went over to the ruined house.

He was glad they'd had this day of conversation. It felt good to talk that much and not be trying to talk his way out of some kind of trouble or something. In a way, it even felt better than talking about the banality of work and school. He felt a lot clearer. He continued to feel a sense of solidarity with Cassie. He couldn't shake the feeling they were in this together for a reason and, perhaps for the first time, he felt truly reassured she didn't want to ditch him somewhere along the way. It also finally occurred to him why she had kept him alive all this time. Why she hadn't sneaked up on him while he was sleeping and buried a rock in his brain.

She felt like she needed him to get out of this. If she offed him, then she feared the doom that came about would be even greater. Or that she would be left to whatever meek existence this place afforded all by herself. Maybe it was better to live out your days with a murderer than it was to live them alone. And maybe that was what this was all about. Maybe there was something in both of them that knew they were going to die and they were simply sparing each other so they would each have someone to die with.

He had also found out that he was completely enamored with Cassie. The situation seemed too perverse to bring it up to her, supposing he could have somehow mustered the courage. He assumed that, because she had nearly been raped, she would most probably never want to have sex again and he didn't think he should be having those thoughts when he should be mourning his parents.

But he was rapidly figuring out that "should" and "ought" were fairly meaningless words these days.

Cassie greedily pulled the grocery produce sack full of oranges out of the crumpled refrigerator and dealt John one of them. With dirty fingernails, he pulled the shiny skin back, relishing the powerful citrus aroma that leaped up at him. He picked at the huge orange and watched lustily as Cassie ate hers. Afterwards, they went to the well and drank from the old tire. He couldn't take his eyes off her.

He watched her get down on her knees, hold her hair back out of her face and drink thirstily from the tire. It would have made a beautiful surrealist photograph, he thought.

He watched the ropy thin muscles in her legs when she walked, noticing her skin had reddened considerably since he'd first seen her.

Occasionally, she would glance at him, as if wondering what part of her body he was studying and John, noticing her gaze, guiltily looked away.

"Well, bucko," she said. "I guess it's into the trunk with you."

"Now? There's like an hour till sunset, at least."

"Better safe than sorry. I have to put the rocks on it all by myself, remember?"

"Oh, yeah."

"Speaking of which, is there a wheelbarrow around here someplace? I don't really want to have to walk those rocks over here one by one."

"There *was* one up around the house."

He began a wandering search, Cassie coming along with him.

After a few minutes, he found it. He would have probably seen it sooner had it not been in such an awkward position. It was over at the edge of the east field, where the field crept in closest to the house. The wheelbarrow's handles were stuck in the ground, the large metal tub facing him.

It took all of his strength to finally dislodge it from the ground.

"There you go," he said.

"Thanks."

Slowly, they walked toward the car, neither of them wanting to be alone.

He opened up the driver's side door and popped the trunk, going around and lifting it up. This car was a lot better than his and he thought it could possibly hold him without the stones, but he knew it would be best to not take any chances. He also hoped it would be a little more comfortable, the trunk a little larger.

Resting his butt against the taillights, he said, "Well, guess I'll see you in the morning, huh?"

"I wish there was some other way. I really do."

She looked at him and at that point he thought she really must be the most empathetic person in the world. Never had he seen eyes that blazed with more kindness. She put a hand on his cheek and leaned toward him, lightly touching her lips to his.

He would have responded with gusto if he knew how. But it probably wasn't gusto she was looking for, anyway. He trembled violently, didn't know what he was feeling, didn't know what to say, so he said, "Thank you."

She giggled at the inappropriateness of the comment and said, "Everything'll be okay. I know it. Trust me."

"I wish *you* could trust *me*," he stammered, his nerves still jangling through him.

"I do, John. What happens at night, that's not you."

"I hope you're right."

"You're still blushing," she pointed out.

"I know. I'd better get into the trunk."

And he did.

In there, strangely, he found comfort. It was cool and dark. He heard the methodical clunk of stones being piled onto the trunk, letting him know she was out there and he was in here. It let him know she was still safe and it made him burn to think the only way for her to be safe was for him to be confined.

He began to wonder if his comfort wasn't maybe just some kind of quiet desperation. Cassie was the last thing he had and if anything happened to her then everything else went away, too. So he comforted himself by saying, "That's not going to happen. That's not going to happen," until he finally drifted off into his dark killing land.

Forty-one

Disgustedly, Cassie underwent another corpse drench with the fetid fluids inside Gregory. This time, it was even more rancid, the coagulated blood making it hard to cover herself.

John's pounding had begun before she'd even reached the field. Luckily, she now knew what it sounded like for the door of a trunk to be ripped from its hinges. Information that, should it happen again, would come in very handy.

The moon hung overhead like a dirty fingernail and she contemplated another night curled up beneath Gregory.

She couldn't do it. There wasn't any way she could see herself doing it again. She had to think of something else. Anything else. Anything besides sleeping under that beast, perversely giving him in death what he would have killed her for in life. No. She wouldn't be doing that again.

Then she had another idea. Equally as sick, sure, but this time at least the sickness couldn't have any personal connotations. It was kind of like the difference between squashing a bug with your hand and running over a cat. One was gross, the other was gross and it could make you feel bad.

She walked over to the pond and contemplated the smaller dead things scattered all around it. Knowing what she intended to do, she picked up a medium-sized frog. Its skin was already shrunken and slightly crispy-looking.

She forced her fingers into its mouth and, with great force, yanked the jaws apart. It made a sickening crunch as its jaws split. She continued to pull the upper jaw, the frog's dry skin splitting down each side. She put the top half of the frog on the ground and, with her boot, tried to scrape as much of the excess blood and tissue from the skin as she could. The gore stuck to the edge of her boot and she noticed how desensitized she'd grown to all this stuff. A week ago she would have been gagging and vomiting. It was simply commonplace now.

Once she thought the frog was sufficiently degored, she bent down and stripped her boot of its lacing.

She stuck the outside of the frog skin up to her nose and mouth, like a surgical mask. Using the stiff tips of her bootlaces, she poked holes through the skin where her nostrils were. Then she put three holes where her mouth was.

She could breathe much better through the frog skin than she had through Gregory and she figured the dead hide would filter out most of her live breath.

This was a gamble, she realized, but she was tired of playing games. She needed to be mobile at night. Otherwise, it would be the same thing every night. Her locking John up and then spending the rest of the night exhausted and hiding. She didn't really think she or John would be able to go on like that for an incredibly long time. Besides, they were going to be out of food soon and the Johnthing had already basically run out of people.

Next she put holes at either end of the skin, putting the tip of the bootlace through the first hole and knotting it. She put the skin up to her face, took the boot lace around the back of her head, pulling until it was sufficiently tight, and tied a knot at the other hole, excess lace dangling down and tickling her neck.

It was a tradeoff. If it worked, she would have the mobility she needed. And the atrocious smell would have to go away after a while. It could be worse. She could have her nose crammed in Gregory's open back.

She went over to the other side of the pond, away from the corpses, and waited, trying desperately not to fall asleep. Her eyes would close, her thoughts fragmenting, and then she would hear John pound on the trunk and immediately be fully awake.

He continued to pound on the trunk. Rather than lessen with fatigue, the sound increased in vehemence. There was the occasional gravelly splash of one of the large stones tumbling off into the driveway.

The last shreds of light slowly left the sky. The darker it became, the more tired Cassie grew. She didn't even know how she could be thinking about sleep right now, but she did. She longed for it. She longed for her comfortable bed at home where she could lie under the covers and look out the window, watching the oak tree in the front yard flutter in the soft glow of the streetlamps.

She could clearly identify the sound of the stones she had placed on the trunk tumble off. She had no idea how many rocks she had piled up there. Fear mounted with each rock that fell off. She would have to leave it to the fear to keep her awake.

She figured John would probably be able to batter himself out. It was just a matter of time. She didn't really have any idea what she would do once he actually freed himself. Maybe she would just run. And run and run and run until there was no place else to run to.

While she waited, something else happened. Something that, although she hadn't expected it, failed to surprise her.

A rustle from the other side of the pond startled her. Her mind wasn't thinking too clearly and she had grown so accustomed to listening for the rocks that it took longer than it should have to realize she was now hearing something else.

She shot up, staring across the pond, the moon affording her only a minimal amount of light to see what was going on. She arced halfway around the east end of the pond, straining her eyes and cursing her sleepiness.

Jerkily, John's father stood up. With the same heavy, ill-jointed awkwardness, he set out walking toward the house.

The first thing that crossed her mind was that he was going to free John. She imagined the Johnthing's heightened sense of hunger and raging fury.

She figured the best thing she could do was to run.

She thought about the place in the woods.

The Devils.

She didn't really know which one she would get. She didn't really care. And maybe some answers would come to her since the woods were where things *really* seemed to happen.

Without another second of hesitation, she charged back toward the woods, wondering if she would be greeted by a dream or a nightmare.

Forty-two

Once Dan had told himself his feelings very well could be wrong, he managed to kind of forget about them for the next couple of nights. Sure, he had driven by the Fresk house at least once a day ever since checking for the first time. So what if he hadn't seen them outside? So what if it looked like their cars hadn't moved at all? He certainly didn't want to be overprotective. He had made that pact with himself the first time he had driven past Gordon's house and seen that everything was okay. He had decided he was not going to call and he was not going to drive up there.

But what kind of a friend are you if you don't?

That was the feeling, the tickle, the voice, whatever the hell it was. Not letting him rest for a second.

Come on, Dan, how long do you think everything can look *normal? You know something happened there. There was a* glow *for Christ's sake! And it wasn't a very* natural *kind of glow either. And all the animals were running away from the very same place you saw the glow.*

Everything is not fine, Dan.

Everything is not fine.

That voice made the hair stand up on his arms.

Everything is not fine.

Aw, fuck it, he thought. What can it hurt to give Gordon a call?

Sitting there at the desk, staring out at the black humid night and listening to the steady drone of the air conditioner, Dan didn't really figure it could hurt at all.

He picked up the phone and dialed.

The phone rang and rang and rang. No one picked up. That didn't really help his feelings much at all. He couldn't exactly remember if he had ever called Gordon's house when no one was at home. In the day of answering machines and voice mail, there seemed to be something almost spooky about a phone just ringing away to an empty room for as long as the caller cared to let it. Maybe, Dan thought, maybe Gordon has call waiting and he was just on the other line like long distance or something. Maybe he was on the internet. Or, Christ, maybe they just weren't home. And maybe, just maybe, they were the last people in America who didn't have an answering machine or voice mail.

Regardless, Dan knew he was not going to go there and knock on their door. A call was one thing, a pop-in was a whole other level of overprotectiveness. That implied the dropper-in wanted to make sure the dropped-in-on was also physically sound. Over the phone, it was entirely possible to speak and sound mostly normal even if one were missing both of one's legs.

So he would just try calling back later.

It couldn't be much later. It was already well after nine and Dan made it a habit to never call people after ten.

He got tired of listening to the radio blather on and the air conditioning started to feel too cold. Now would be a good time for a walk. He liked his evening strolls. It allowed him to get out and enjoy nature, the whole reason he had taken this job to begin with.

He packed up his pipe and got it going, tossing the match into the ashtray and heading out into the night. He took a drag from his pipe and stared up at the sky. He had never been anywhere where he could see more stars than he could from right here. It was a little breathtaking every time he really thought about it and he didn't really know why it wasn't something he did more often.

He knew what he was really doing was killing time until he could go back in and redial Gordon's number, but he didn't want to admit that to himself.

Okay, so his walk really wasn't much of a walk. He kind of walked around the station parking lot and took in the smell of the sweet clover, listening to the susurrating insects, the giddy rubber band sounds of the frogs, the hoarse laments of the bullfrogs and the occasional breeze blowing through the trees—a sound he found as soothing as the waves on a beach.

Then, from out of nowhere, he got another one of his feelings. This one was so strong there wasn't any way it could have been wrong. It closely resembled a panic attack, more so than any of his previous feelings.

Things were not right at the Fresk house. He was sure of that. But there was more. Jesus, so many things were shooting through his head he didn't know which of the thoughts he should try and latch onto. There was much more than what was happening at the Fresk household. Whatever it was, it was of monumental importance.

So, when Dan saw Gordon Fresk shamble into the light cast by the security lamp in the parking lot, he assumed the worst.

"Gordon?" Dan called. He saw visions of rape and torture, the whole family locked up inside that house ever since the storm. Gordon had finally been the one to escape and now he was coming to the one place where he knew he could count on help.

"Gordon?" he called again.

This was weird. Why wasn't Gordon answering him?

Gordon continued coming toward him. Dan walked toward Gordon, thinking his friend limped more than walked, as though he had been seriously injured.

Dan smelled something foul—Gordon's decay—before realizing whatever Gordon had undergone, it wasn't normal.

But Dan didn't even think about drawing his gun. What could have happened to Gordon that would make him want to hurt Dan?

No, Dan told himself. He was just slightly lost and confused and something very very bad had obviously happened to him.

A rock hit Dan in the head and he went down, unconscious. His feelings could never have predicted what would happen to him and, if they had predicted it, the rational part of Dan would have dismissed the idea as completely ludicrous.

Forty-three

The thing that used to be Gordon stood over Dan, looking down at him. There wasn't any recognition in Gordon's eyes. There wasn't any sadness. This was Gordon the shell. Gordon the puppet. He now acted according to something else, merely a mass of tissue and innards, some of which hung out the wounds in his back. Whatever thoughts he had now were not his own.

Stiffly, he bent down and touched the big man that lay on the asphalt. Gordon had done a good job. Something inside of him told him this. The man on the ground would not be moving for a long time but he wasn't dead, like Gordon. The blood still flowed beneath his skin, his heart still beat. The thing that was in the car would want this man like he had once wanted Gordon. Gordon understood he could no longer be useful for food, but he could be useful in this way, in bringing food back to the thing in the car.

Only the dead can leave. That was what the woman had told him. He wasn't exactly sure when she had told him this. There seemed to be two of him. There was the Gordon that had once occupied this body, and he had left upon death. And then there was the dead body and now there was him, here to occupy the dead body.

175

He wasn't entirely sure who *he* was.

He knew he could only move at night.

He knew he listened to everything the woman said, whispering things in the back of his head.

And he knew he was incredibly strong.

He looked at the man, crumpled and bleeding on the ground, and knew he could pick him up with no problem whatsoever. So, stiffly, the thing that used to be Gordon bent and picked up Dan Wrigley, slinging him across his shoulder. He knew he had to work quickly before the big man woke up because, even though the thing that used to be Gordon was strong, he was also deteriorating and didn't know how well he would be able to hold up if the big man attacked him.

Gordon moved quickly along the road.

He also knew he was not like everyone else. In other words, he knew nobody was supposed to see him carrying this man down the road. It only took him a few minutes to reach the gravel driveway but, once he did, once he crossed the threshold, he felt stronger. More in his element. He could hear the woman, whispering in the back of his head, telling him where to take the man.

He reached the car that harbored the Johnthing and sat the big man down on the gravel of the driveway. Then he removed the stones from the car's trunk and tossed them off to the side. Like the big man, these stones weighed absolutely nothing to him. He could have probably picked up the car and dumped the stones off just as easily.

Minutes later, after all the stones were removed, he went to the driver's side door and popped the trunk.

Inside the trunk, the Johnthing lay curled around himself, whimpering. Whimpering because he was so hungry his senses were dulled and he couldn't catch a whiff of food in the air. Something in his head told him there should be food. He vaguely remembered something from the previous night—something he couldn't catch. Something he had saved for tonight.

John's thoughts were rudimentary at best. He knew it was impossible for that other piece of food to leave but there was no way for him to search out this area by scent alone. And being so hungry, crazily hungry, there was no way he could concentrate on that scent.

But there was another thing in front of him. Something of even lesser intelligence. Something that stank so heavily of death John wanted to sink back into the trunk. But this thing was here to help John.

Somewhere within him, possibly from that other person who occupied his flesh, the Johnthing remembered something that sounded like, "Only the dead can leave." Try as he might, the Johnthing had absolutely no idea what that meant. Even taken individually, the words were only sounds in his head. Useless.

Gordon sensed the look of understanding coming from the Johnthing. He bent down and dipped his fingers in the big man's blood, bringing them, glistening wet, to hold beneath the Johnthing's nose. The Johnthing licked Gordon's fingers greedily, snarled, and bit them off. Gordon did not feel anything. The Johnthing, choking on the taste of death, spit Gordon's fingers back out.

But now he caught the scent of the living blood, it fevered through his brain, blossomed in his stomach.

He hopped out of the trunk and fell upon the big man on the driveway's gravel.

Gordon, knowing his job was done, shambled back over to the pond, where all the other dead things were.

Under the cold glare of the moon, the Johnthing continued to seek his sustenance from Dan Wrigley.

Forty-four

By the time she reached the woods, Cassie was shaking and out of breath. Had John's father seen her run in this direction? Maybe he was resurrected to serve as John's eyes.

This was something completely new and different to worry about. Now, not only would something with an incredibly strong sense of smell be hunting her, but she also had to worry about not being seen, which would probably be a little easier than not being smelled. Of course, it would now be possible for them to cover twice as much ground. So not only did she have to worry about the Johnthing, she had to worry about zombies, too.

She was terrified.

Before entering the woods, she paused, silently hoping John's brother would be there. She didn't know why he comforted her. Hell, she didn't even know if he was real or not.

She crept into the dead woods, the twigs and dry leaves snapping beneath her boots. With her magnificent dream still etched into her head, she had almost forgotten how dark the woods actually were. But she could smell it in front of her, something like the radiating essence of the dream. It was the smell of rich, dark earth moistened by rain. The woody smell of tree bark. The ripeness of spring. The beauty of life.

And then she was in it. If everything she had experienced before had been a dream, then the dream was back. In front of her, a green clearing. Elliot stood in the middle.

The sensation Cassie experienced was not only completely visual. An all-pervading calm also invaded her body. The blood pounding in her ears was gone. The rasp of her breath was gone. And there was something else, too. Outside this area, there was some kind of unavoidable buzz that rang in her ears but, in here, it was gone.

Elliot motioned for her to come and sit on a huge rock, half-submerged into the ground.

She did so, meeting Elliot's eyes. They were the most tranquil eyes she had ever seen. Rarely did eyes actually seem to radiate. Cassie looked into Elliot's eyes and it felt like she was drinking his calm.

"Hello," Elliot said, his voice low and soothing.

"Hello," Cassie said.

"Are there questions you have for me?"

"Yes. Many," Cassie said, although she couldn't exactly remember what they were.

"And you seek the answers?"

"Yes."

"I will provide you with all the answers I can. Some of them, I'm afraid, you will find inadequate. Some of them I may not even begin to answer. First of all, let me warn you—you must, after tonight, stay away from this area."

"Why?" she asked, feeling kind of dumb.

"Let me begin by telling you about the area outside of this circle. Maybe my explanation will answer some of your other questions along the way."

Cassie nodded her head, captivated by Elliot's eyes. They were blue, the most beautiful color blue she'd ever seen, but they seemed to contain a depth that made her think they reached all the way back to some foreign blue sky.

That was it, Cassie thought. That was the striking thing about Elliot's eyes. She remembered John talking about his dream where he stood there in the woods and saw, not only the woods, but some place entirely different.

"The area outside this circle, and by circle I mean this immediate clearing, the area you and John are confined to, is called a Tantalus. It is an area that corresponds with areas of other places. Other worlds. I don't know how to explain it, exactly. I'm sure you've heard the theory before. There are areas where the walls that border your world and other worlds are thinner. Magical people, your kind of people, once inhabited this area. They didn't have what you would consider technology. If they needed food, then they begged their gods for the right amount of rain. If they were sick, they summoned their gods to come and take the sickness away. There were others who summoned different gods. Maybe, for whatever reason, they wanted to afflict another member of their tribe with disease or possibly even death. When the gods of these people were called upon, they came. But what these people thought were gods were actually from those other worlds.

"Are you getting this so far?"

Cassie nodded her head and said, "I think so." It occurred to her that, if she and John had not decided to stop thinking rationally, she wouldn't believe any of this stuff.

"These people from the other worlds, they were mostly good.

"And people of the sort that made John the way he is. Me the way I am. So I guess they're my people now. The Devils. We're mainly only called that because we're different. Sure, some of us do terrible things, but those are the only ones people choose to recognize. The relationship has always been symbiotic. Your people gave us everything we gave them. And then, one day, your people were all but gone. Rather, their ways of magic were gone. They decided to put their energies toward something more practical—the gods of industry and agriculture. But the connection between this world and ours always remained. Most of us would never abuse this connection. Occasionally we will send one of our people here so they can better appreciate their own world when they come back.

"Our world, like yours, is a very vast place. It contains many many different types of people. Some of them are good. Some of them are bad. Most of them are a little bit of both. Same as here.

"These Devils who've done this to you come from a very dark part of our world. I do not know much about them or their country. I know the sun never shines there and they want to take something from your world. I know they are evil. Their own souls, their own lives, are so polluted they seek those essentials from others—lives and souls. My people have been waiting for this to happen. There's a dark fire that burns. It is the gateway. It is currently in the hands of the good. It hasn't always been that way. And the Dark Fire has a way of making good people go bad. Possessing something that powerful. The woman who has prescribed the Tantalus that surrounds you and John is named Ilya. She lost her companion Ernst. She is very powerful but, without Ernst, she's incomplete. However, she is also very upset. She has planted something in John. Something he's supposed to give birth to. She is planning to take that and use it as Ernst's vessel so they can be reunited.

"And then she plans on connecting the two worlds even more than they already are. She wants everyone from her world to be able to come here.

"This would be catastrophic for both worlds.

"The Devils are already here. They always have been. But there aren't that many of them and most of them would like to remain undetected. But Ilya is powerful. Sometimes, especially when she's at her strongest, she can control them. At best, you and John would destroy Ilya. John, like me, is forever changed. For those of us that still draw breath and have blood pumping through us, that's the only way we can ever return to normal. At the very least, you have to stop what's in John from getting out. And if it *does* get out, you have to destroy it. Whatever it takes."

Cassie didn't know how to process this information. She needed clarity. "I know you have questions," Elliot said. "And this might be the last time we meet so you'll need to ask them now."

Forty-five

"Okay," Cassie tried to shake the confusion from her head. "So what *are* the Devils?"

"You name it. Originally, they came from another place. Another world. Parts of that world are beautiful but parts are dying. Those who are still there are either trapped or monsters."

"So they're monsters?"

"Not all of them. The most powerful are in spirit form. They can inhabit whoever they choose. Some of them do this without the person they're inhabiting even noticing it. Many times these people go on to do great things because of this. Sometimes the Devils consume the soul of the body they're inhabiting. Take it over and use it as a puppet. Consequently, many of these people are very powerful and do many horrible things. some are basically what you would call vampires. This, I'm afraid, is what John is on the road to becoming. He's been bitten. Just like I was so, again, the only way to return is to destroy the person who bit him. Who is, as it happens, the same person who bit me."

"Ilya."

"Exactly."

"So you...?"

"I need blood to live. Yes. I will not age beyond the age I was when bitten. I can tolerate sunlight but I don't really like it and would probably get sick if I went to the beach or something. But I don't kill people. And if I know John as well as I think I do, I don't think he will either... If he can help it."

Cassie wondered if he already knew about their parents. She comforted herself by thinking he *had* to know. She didn't want to be the one to tell him."

"So... why does John become what he becomes?"

"You have to stop thinking about your biology. They put something like a seed in his body. That seed needs food to grow. When they planted the seed, John stopped being entirely human. Now, he is human for half the day. During the night, he is merely a puppet, a vessel to bring this seed food so it can grow. At night, his body no longer functions the way a human body does. It can do things you would think of as impossible. But it has its limitations."

"It's blind, isn't it?"

"Yes. Everyone from that other place is blind except for the very elite. Many people say they are blind because there is nothing of beauty to look upon in their land."

"And why have they done this to John?"

"Because they would like to see all worlds destroyed except their own... and he was there. In the wrong place at the wrong time..."

"So, through John, they are hoping to… what, kill everyone on earth?"

"Something like that. I imagine they would keep a good many of you as slaves. Their main goal is chaos. If you have a world of cannibals, they can only survive for so long. Eventually they consume themselves."

"Is there any way to get whatever it is inside of John out of him?"

"I'm almost certain."

"Do you know how we could do that?"

He lowered his head and shook it, looking nearly ashamed.

"Without John, the demon dies?"

"That is my understanding. However, if John dies, it can still escape."

"So what happened out there? Why's everything dead?"

"That's nature out of balance. That section of earth was briefly exposed to our world, maybe for just a second or two, and the effect was devastating. Our worlds do not mesh very well."

"Did it have something to do with the storm?"

"It had everything to do with the storm. A storm is one form of chaos. It is the ideal time for these things to act. The more violent the storm, the better. The storm helped camouflage their entrance."

"But these things can be destroyed?"

"Yes. Well, that's not exactly true. They can be stopped. They can be pushed back into their own world and contained. When that happens, if that happens, the Tantalus needs to be closed. This will prevent anyone else entering through it. Only, make sure you are on this side when it closes, or else you will find yourself stuck in their world. I'm afraid you wouldn't last too long there."

Cassie shivered. "And how do I keep John from destroying me or himself?"

"I wish I could answer that."

Cassie shook her head, confused. "This is a lot to take in. I do have one more question and it might end up helping a lot."

"I'll answer anything I can."

"There's a book and John seems to think it has a lot to do with what's happening."

"Well, it doesn't have anything to do with what's happening."

"But you've heard of this book?"

Elliot smiled. "Most of us have. It has nothing to do with what's happening to you. However, for a work of pure fiction written by a man of questionable talent, it gives a pretty accurate description of some things that have happened."

"So John isn't wrong?"

"I hesitate to say that. It is, in the end, a work of fiction. By no means should it be used as any kind of guide."

"But Ilya and Ernst and the Dark Fire..."

"Yes. Ilya is the name of the woman who did this to us. Ernst is... well, it's quite possible that Ernst is what's in John. I'm sure the Dark Fire and the Low Church exist but I've never seen them." He was silent for a moment. "And there's something else about it. It's not a particularly sophisticated book by any stretch of the imagination but when I read it, I couldn't help thinking of it as some kind of puzzle. But I haven't figured it out yet."

Cassie sat and stared sullenly at the ground. Elliot spoke softly, lifting Cassie's chin with a gentle hand. "I'm going to miss it here," he said. "But it's too dangerous for me to stay."

"Thank you for your help," Cassie said. "Thank you for everything you've told me."

"But it feels like I haven't told you anything."

"No. Really. I think the talk was valuable." And even as she said it, Cassie felt how truly inadequate her remark was. She knew she couldn't even come close to understanding what was going on.

"Since becoming... what I've become, I'm not without my own powers. If you stay in this immediate area where everything is alive, you'll be safe. It won't last past tomorrow, but you should be able to get a few hours rest. But you need to remember to never come back here. Not until this has passed."

Cassie nodded obediently.

"And you need to remember something else, also. As of right now, you and John are the most important people to the human race. I know it may not seem like it but whatever decisions you make will influence humankind forever."

Again, Cassie nodded, trying not to feel the impact of what Elliot had just said. Trying not to feel the impact, trying to shut it out like she had so many other times and still feeling it blaze up within her.

Cassie raised her head to say thank you but Elliot was gone, back to whatever beautiful place he had come from.

She realized she was still wearing the frog mask and, having faith in what Elliot said, tore the mask off. She couldn't believe it. A night without worry. This might be just the thing she needed, she thought. Just the thing to recharge her batteries and bring whatever frail plans she and John had to fruition. She slumped down to the ground and let a deep, dreamless sleep wrap its water arms around her body and mind.

Forty-six

Cassie woke up just before dawn and made the trek back to the pond in the lingering dark. Before leaving the circle, she refastened the frog mask.

On her way, she found herself feeling nearly carefree. She really hadn't slept that long but, just being able to go to sleep knowing she would be able to wake up when she wanted to did a lot for her. It had been the first period of time, however small, when she had been free from worry. She knew it was impossible for the feeling to last but, for the moment, she felt really good. Beneath the still-dark sky, the cornfield passed quickly below her feet on the way to the pond, the energy propelling her walk a foreign feeling.

She reached the meadow and, unexpectedly, nearly stumbled onto the Johnthing. And he wasn't a sleeping Johnthing, either. She pulled to a stop just a few feet away. It was enough to see the details of what the beast was doing, even though the first glow of the day had yet to light the sky.

Beneath John lay a new corpse. John's father had resumed his rightfully recumbent position back on the ground.

The carcass beneath John was the worst yet. Cassie wondered if it was someone John knew. *Had there actually been someone else on the property (the Tantalus)?* she wondered.

Even though she didn't really want to watch, she did. She told herself to run, but her legs wouldn't move. So she stood and watched as John burrowed his mouth farther into the man's torso, spreading it apart with his hands. She heard him lapping at the innards, sucking organs up into his mouth.

Then he was finished.

The Johnthing stood up and began walking away. He sniffed at the air around him and turned back, coming toward Cassie.

What if Elliot was a dream?

Run! Get the hell away!

But she couldn't do that. If Elliot had been a dream then Cassie couldn't believe anything he had said and if she couldn't believe anything he had said then she really didn't see a need to continue. If the entire human race wasn't involved then maybe it was best if John just devoured her and was done with it.

She felt his nose press up against her leg. He had dropped onto all fours. He ran his nose up the inside of her leg and sniffed under her skirt, where her scent was the strongest.

She tensed, wondering if she would feel the claws or the teeth first. Wondering what it would feel like to be devoured while conscious, to have her stomach and lungs ground between those teeth.

She closed her eyes, thinking that would somehow make it less painful. Anxiously, she stood as still as possible. She felt something on her leg and looked down.

John licked her skin and gagged, his tongue grazing along the dried gore.

But an elliptical spot of her pale flesh was now exposed beneath her gore drench.

He licked again, this time wrapping his huge hands around her legs. She felt the tip of a claw on the back of her thigh. She shivered violently.

He growled and closed his mouth around her leg. She closed

her eyes, knowing this was probably it, and opened them in astonishment when she didn't feel his teeth rip through her flesh.

Looking down, she saw him curled up on the ground.

From behind her the first bloody rays of the sun streaked across the horizon.

She bent down and put a hand on his face, changed back to the John she liked, and said, "You wouldn't hurt *me* would you?" Then she laughed, finally allowing her tears of terror to roll down her cheeks.

Taking deep breaths along the way, she went to the pond to wash herself off.

Forty-seven

John heard the sickeningly sloshy sounds before he could open his eyes. The sounds incorporated themselves into the last shreds of a dream he couldn't remember, maybe just some remnant of his nocturnal life.

Not alarming him in the least, he contemplated the sounds. Wet and spongy, with something hard in there. Not altogether unpleasant. But foreign. Different. He couldn't think of what could possibly be making that sound.

Then the entire situation flooded back to him.

Where was he?

His heart hammered.

He opened his eyes and stared up at blue sky.

This certainly wasn't the trunk.

But if he got out of the trunk, then…

As he scrambled to his knees, he shouted her name.

"Cassie! Cassie!"

"I'm right here," she said.

Eyes still adjusting, he looked at her. It took him a second longer than it should have to realize she was doing something unusual, the days were so filled with unusual. She was covered in blood up to her elbows. Her dingy white shirt was also spattered with blood.

"Why are you slamming that rock into my dad's leg?"

Frantic, Cassie shouted, "Because he can walk!"

John's first response was to laugh at her but then he thought better of it. He paced around in a small circle. The idea suddenly hit him that she was probably going through a lot more than he was. He had the physical stuff, true. His body expended the energy to mutate and change forms each night. He had the hunt. But what about the emotional turmoil Cassie had undergone each night? She had to remain ever vigilant and there was always the chance she could be the hunted. Not to mention she had not been eating nearly as well as he had.

He bent down next to her and put his hand on her damp back as she hoisted the rock above her head and slammed it into his father's upper thigh, the rock clumping bone and sending a spray of blood out from the radius of the impact.

He noticed the other body.

"Oh God," he said. "How did Dan Wrigley get here?"

Cassie tossed the rock over into the pond out of disgust and buried her weeping eyes into her bloody hands.

"It's okay." He rubbed his hand up and down in between her shoulders, feeling the nubs of her spine beneath his palm. When he realized he was enjoying it too much, he quickly pulled his hand away.

"We need to get their legs off," she mumbled through sticky cottonmouth.

"Okay."

"There's so much we need to talk about but I'm so fucking tired my skin is crawling. I was okay this morning. I felt so refreshed this morning but I've been doing *this* ever since dawn and now I'm so... damn tired."

"It's okay," he said. "Why don't you go over to the shade tree. I'll... remove their legs. I won't even ask why until you've had your nap."

"Last night…"

"No," he cut her off. "You need to sleep. It's the least you can do for looking over my ass every night."

He put an arm around her back and pulled her up.

"Come on," he said. "I'll walk you over there."

They walked over into the backyard, John keeping his arm around her small waist, and Cassie lay down in the grass, falling immediately asleep. She was probably half-asleep on the walk over. He stood over top of her, watching her, wanting her. He knew it wasn't right. He shouldn't even be thinking about sex, but there she was, that skirt reaching just down her thighs. It occurred to him he could slide the skirt up just a little and see something he'd never seen in the flesh before. But he couldn't. He wouldn't be able to look at her without guilt inscribed all over his face.

He went in search of something else to do besides dwell on intangibles.

Cut their legs off, huh?

He knew he was going to do it. So what if it didn't make any sense. It couldn't do any harm, either. Could it?

He went over to the wreckage of the house and began sifting through. If his luck was good, he'd run across the set of kitchen knives that would make the delegging go that much more smoothly.

He looked for what was probably a half an hour that felt like three, scrambling around on the heap of rocks, turning stones over, seeing things he thought *might be something*, but when he came upon it it was just a splinter of wood from a bedframe or the cabinets or something else equally useless. Sweat ran into his eyes, stinging them. The sun was high and hot and today was a little more humid than the past several days.

He quit the mess of rocks and went down to get a drink of water. He drank until his stomach hurt and went over to check on Cassie again.

Her blood-covered arms were crossed behind her head and her shirt was raised, the hems fallen to either side, leaving her perfectly white, flat stomach exposed. While he stood there and watched her, his belly full, the nightmare temporarily behind him, he didn't care if they ever got out of here. Being in Cassie's company made the experience somehow worthwhile. The girls at school that looked like her, John knew, were the same girls that laughed at him when he couldn't see them. When he couldn't ogle them.

Other thoughts shot around his head. *What if you don't ever get out of here? What if tonight's the last night Cassie's even alive? What if you let this moment get away? She kissed you last night, if you don't remember. You had those lips on yours. You had that soft, pale flesh beneath your hands. What if she dies tonight or you both die tonight and you never feel anything more than that kiss. Being inside of her would be like kissing Heaven. You know that, don't you?*

Yes, he agreed. *But she needs rest.*

And he tore himself away from that image of perfection lying at his feet.

He went back to the rock pile, this time with the intention of finding a rock sharp enough to do the deed rather than looking for a knife. Without much searching, he found one that looked like an enlarged arrowhead. He took the rock over to the field, wishing Cassie were awake to do this with him.

Forty-eight

As he twisted the crushed and splintery remains of his father's leg from his body, John wondered, *Why are you doing this, again?*

He didn't know. He told himself he shouldn't even be thinking about it. Every morning was like opening his eyes on the wreckage created by that other life. Without Cassie to explain things to him, he had no answers to his questions.

Like why Wrigley was there.

The only thing he could think of was that the man was unfortunate enough to be in this area when the storm hit and that other John had finally sniffed him out. After all, if Wrigley worked in forestry, it was entirely possible he would have been able to go a few days without much trouble.

John looked at the small body line-up in front of him.

Did she mean *all* the legs?

There were seven more. He thought it probably took him an hour just to finish what Cassie had started. There had to be a better way. He wouldn't have enough time in the day to remove the rest of their legs. His mom and dad were the thinnest of the bunch. John figured that it would take him much longer to remove Dan's and Gregory's legs.

Of course, he thought. *Why not burn the bodies?*

Hell, why not burn this whole fucking area? Burn themselves right out.

He let the rock drop and went about dragging the other bodies over to the fat one. The fat one, "Gregory," looked a lot worse than the other ones. John thought about him being all over Cassie. He thought about what Gregory tried to do to her. If John had a knife, he thought it would be fun to cut off his dick and shove it in his mouth. Gregory was the only one there who he thought he might secretly enjoy removing the legs of.

He began to think this would be a good way to surprise Cassie. He would make a small pyre and set everything ablaze. Then he would roll a joint and have it waiting for her when she got up.

He moved as fast as he could, running around, picking up any pieces of dead wood he could find. There were some good-sized planks from the barn that were scattered around. He removed some others that hung loosely from the barn's frame.

In the time it would have taken him to remove one leg, he had a pyre assembled that was as tall as he was.

He stuffed all the holes and gaps with hay from the barn.

The lighter he and Cassie had used yesterday was in his shorts pocket. He flicked the roller and held it to one of the lowest sections of hay. It went up with a crackle and spread like insanity, the orange flame blackening and devouring the wood beneath it. Everything was so dry.

Feeling good, he walked to his dad's car and fished out the bag of pot. He wasn't exactly sure why they had put it back exactly where it had come from. It took him about a half an hour to roll the stupid thing but, when finished, he was impressed with his handiwork. Putting the joint in his pocket with the lighter, he crossed over to the well to get some water. After he drank his fill, he got another tireful and took it over to Cassie.

He reached down and, putting his hand on her shoulder, gently shook her. He resisted the urge to run his hands all over her body.

"I'm awake," she said.

"Here, drink."

She drank from the tire while he lit the joint and took a lungful of smoke. When she finished drinking, he leaned over her, putting his mouth over hers and blew the smoke into her mouth. She resisted at first and then hungrily pulled it in. He pulled away and watched as she blew the smoke out.

"Mmm," she said. "Wake and bake."

"And," he said, handing the joint to her. "I took care of all those pesky bodies."

"Good. You got all their legs off?"

"Better than that… I burned them."

She coughed out a mouth of smoke. "You *what*?"

"I burned them. Actually, I'm burning them right now. Can't you smell it?"

"Shit, John. That's not good."

"What do you mean?"

She lay back, resigned. "Hell, it doesn't matter. Might as well get our buzz on before I tell you."

They passed the joint back and forth, smoking it until it was too small to hold.

She surprised him by putting her head on his lap and looking up at him.

"I've got a lot more stuff to tell you."

"Long night, huh?"

"Oh, yeah."

She told him she'd seen Elliot. She told him what Elliot had said. She told him about his zombiefied dad, sent to catch his dinner. She even told him about the gore drenching and the frog mask and then he understood why he shouldn't have burned the bodies.

All of it had a cataclysmic effect on John. He saw all the doors closing in front of him until he couldn't think of any reasonable outlet.

"If it's what we need, that storm had better come soon," he said.

"Maybe we should do a rain dance."

"That's not a bad idea."

"You start."

He stood up and stumbled. He seemed to be a lot more stoned than he was yesterday. He had no idea what he was supposed to do.

"What'm I supposed to do?" he asked.

"Do whatever you want. You're trying to make the rain come. Maybe you should chant or something."

He turned around, hopped from foot to foot and started laughing.

"Shouldn't I say something? 'Abracadabra' or something like that?"

"It doesn't matter. You have to *feel* it, man." Cassie laughed.

She stood up and turned herself toward the west. Then she threw herself down onto her knees, looked at the sky and began yapping loudly. She looked over her shoulder at John, shuffling around behind her.

"Come on," she said. "You're too uptight. The more you just go with it and do what you want to do, the better everything'll feel."

She stood up and leaped toward the sky. "Rain!" she shouted. "Storms! Lightning! Thunder!"

She grabbed the book from where it had been lying on the ground, tossed it at him, and said, "Here, read something from this."

John thought back to the night of the storm. He thought about all the energy that surged through him, how he wanted the storm to come down and claim him. He supposed, in a way, it had. He watched Cassie jump up, higher and higher, her skirt flapping up in back, allowing him a fleeting glimpse of her bare ass. He moved beside her, joining in her jumping. She shouted out the same words over and over until it finally became something like a chant.

"Rain!

"Storms!

"Lightning!

"Thunder!"

John opened the book to the middle and began reading the words backward. "Thgin tsol a ot stuohs rieht gnimaercs ezalb tcefrep a ni pu tnew yeht dna hctam a dessot eh neht!"

They ran over to the pasture, John behind Cassie, shouting, leaping and laughing.

Reaching the fire, they danced around it, in and out of the acrid flesh smoke. He couldn't take his eyes off her, her lank black hair bouncing up and down, spinning out around her head. The smooth white skin of her legs, the smooth white of her lower back and stomach.

Mixed with the heat of the day, it was sweltering next to the fire. Within minutes they were both drenched in sweat. He had to keep going, matching Cassie. He couldn't think about anything anymore except the rhythm, Cassie's running skipping dance, the hoarse shouting of the chant, the crackling energy of the fire.

They danced around the fire, ran into each other, and fell down on the hot earth.

He scrambled toward Cassie, hungry for her. She met him, their mouths grinding into one another. He explored her mouth with his tongue. It tasted like exotic spices, something unreal and unknown. He wanted to put his hands all over her at once—the firmness of her small breasts beneath the wet shirt, the fragility of her neck, the thin perfection of her arms, his hands nearly able to encircle them.

He pulled away from her mouth, wanting to see what was in front of him.

The look in her eyes was a look he had never seen before, not even in the movies. He guessed it was pure lust, but it penetrated into him, stiffening him further, swelling some feeling beneath his skin.

She put her hand on the bulge in his shorts.

"Let's make the storm," she said. "Let's make the storm."

"Are you sure…" She cut him off with another kiss, her momentum carrying him backward until she was on top of him, her weight resting on his waist.

He reached out and pulled her shirt open, eyes resting on the dark-nippled breasts atop a ladder of ribs. She moved down, grinding her crotch against him. Then she scooted down until she rested on his thighs. She reached down, unbuttoning and unzipping his shorts, sliding them down. He shook with nervousness and desire and revelation. He lifted up her skirt, reached in and felt the hot moisture of her bare sex.

She moved forward, sliding herself against him, giving him only a taste of what it would feel like inside.

She stood up and completely removed her shirt, tossing it into the fire. She unfastened her skirt and let it fall to her ankles, bending down and tossing that into the fire. Then she pulled off her boots and did the same with them.

"Now you," she said.

He obeyed, removing his clothes as quickly as possible and tossing them into the fire.

They moved closer to each other almost like two combatants.

They kissed again. He ran his hands down her back, cupping her ass, letting his fingertips brush the perimeter of her anus. He felt it draw tight. With her arms around his neck, he picked her up by the back of her thighs and placed her on the ground. He moved his hands behind her knees, lifting her legs up and spreading them. He looked into her eyes that never seemed to close and didn't want to look away. By locking stares it was like they were both able to feel everything inside the other person.

She reached down and guided him into her. He bent over her, pressing down on her, wanting to absorb her as she absorbed him.

Rhythmically, he thrust into her, feeling the fire draw closer to them, making it so hot it burned.

But neither of them wanted to move.

The flames licked up the dead grass around them, lapped at the two naked bodies, encircling them.

He continued to thrust. She shoved her hips toward him.

The slap of skin.

The crackle of the fire.

The screams.

The flames ignited on their hair, dripping down their bodies, consuming them.

He thrust toward a pleasure that was only seconds away.

They both climaxed, shaking away burnt skin as he came into her.

He felt something painful. Something ripping tearing crawling out of his body and into hers.

And then the flame and the screaming fear consumed all other thought.

Forty-nine

Was he in the woods?

John certainly thought it was the woods but they didn't seem familiar.

These woods seemed deeper, darker, more sinister. The trees were larger, blotting the moon from the sky. They leaned in all different directions as though each of them were involved in a struggle to reach the ground. The wind whispered through the woods and the trees groaned.

He continued walking, going deeper and deeper into the woods, moving on soft dream feet.

Where was Cassie?

Where the hell was *he?*

What the fuck was happening?

Maybe this is the end, he thought. He hoped it was. He wanted to get everything over with. A conclusion, something definite, was more important to him than staying alive at this point.

Up ahead, in the deep murk of the woods, he saw a fire glowing. Maybe the fire was huge and very far away. Or maybe it was a small fire nearby. It didn't matter. It was something alive in the death of this murk. It was something to move toward.

Fifty

Cassie watched John go up in a whoosh of fire after he came into her. The fire surged one last time through her, as if to cleanse her, and then retreated back to the larger fire, where it burned with a bluish intensity.

She stood up and doubled over. There was an added weight in her stomach. Her crotch was a bloody mess and her first absurd thought was that she had started her period.

But she knew it wasn't that time.

She remembered the thing that came from John and crawled into her, the pain worse than the flames scraping at her skull with punitive fingernails.

She surveyed the field around her for as far as she could. It was dark now. Something had happened.

She was lost. She had no idea what to do. Somewhere along the line, she had released all control. Up to this point, she reckoned, things had been relatively easy. As absurd as it was, she and John had worked out a kind of bizarre routine. Survival had been the only name of the game. They each knew what they had to do. Lock the Johnthing away before it got dark and play the waiting game for the rest of the night. Most importantly, she had always known where John was.

But today, something had gone terribly wrong.

By burning the bodies, he had taken any defense mechanism she had. And that didn't matter because it was dark now and she hadn't done anything to protect herself. She stood beneath the sky, naked, wrapping her arms around herself and trying to think linear thoughts so madness couldn't creep in with its disorienting parade but all of her thoughts begged madness.

What's inside of you?

Are you even awake?

When are you *going to change?*

This is a dream. Dream.

She wanted to tell herself it wasn't a dream but, if it wasn't a dream, then it was death, right? The fire would have consumed her as easily as it had consumed John, right? She could remember how the fire sizzled at her, bubbled her skin, ran up and down her nerve endings.

Then she remembered the thing John had told her about that first vision he had.

"Only the dead can leave," the woman had told him. "Only the dead can leave."

Gordon had left to go get the other guy and bring him back.

Was there a way to find out if she was dead or not?

Cassie was sure there was.

She walked slowly toward the west end of the pasture, toward the road. This time, she *wanted* that wall to hold her back. She wanted to know she was still alive and there was still something to fight for. She didn't want to be another dead thing.

Fifty-one

As John drew closer to the fire, he could make out the shapes surrounding it.

Some grain of thought told him he shouldn't go any farther. That he shouldn't be around those people. Those soul suckers.

But he continued onward, unable to stop himself.

And he didn't really want to stop himself anyway. He wanted to confront these people. He didn't care who they were. He didn't care where they came from. They were responsible for him living the last twelve years of his life in fear. They were responsible for Elliot's disappearance. They were responsible for the death of both of his parents. These people needed to be destroyed and John wanted to be the person to destroy them.

When he broke into the clearing, they were all standing in front of the fire in a half-moon shape. Slowly, they moved toward him, their half-moon becoming a circle that surrounded him. The woman emerged from the circle and stood very close to him. She leaned in as if to whisper in his ear. Instead of whispering, she screamed, "You lost our child!"

The scream sent him to his knees.

"I… didn't know." He couldn't think of anything else to say.

"You are ours now." The woman bent over him.

He looked at her and wondered how he could have ever thought she was beautiful. Her skin was drawn too tightly over her face. A crazed look glistened in her eyes. Grayish, stringy hair hung down in her face. Her breath stank.

"Fuck you," he said.

The woman circled behind him and kicked him in the back of the head. He rolled over onto his back and stared up, the canopy of the trees swimming around the swollen moon. *Yes*, he thought, *it has to be a dream because, back in Realityland, that moon isn't even half-full.*

The woman got down on her knees beside him.

"Luckily," she said. "We know exactly where our child has gone. Look at the moon, John."

John, who was already looking at the moon, saw an image appear. It was Cassie, stumbling through the darkness, looking blind and lost.

"Leave her alone."

"You should relax, John. The macho thing doesn't suit you. I'll tell you exactly what's going to happen to her. She's going to continue doing what you've been doing while the baby grows and matures. And when it's ready to taste the world, it will tear itself out of her and leave behind something totally unrecognizable. But, look on the bright side, it could be you."

"Fuck you."

"Of course, you have your bad fate, too. See, now that our child is in that girl, we can put another one in you. Would you like that? You remember what it was like, don't you? Wouldn't you like to do that again?"

By way of an answer, John made a fist and drove it into the woman's face. Her skin split open as easily as a rotten apple, sliding back to reveal the gray skull beneath it. The woman staggered back and stood up. She reached up and removed the rest of her face, letting it drop from her fingers in glistening chunks.

He stood up and stumbled back into a gigantic tree.

"Where are you going to run, John?" the woman asked. "You don't even have any idea where you are. Look around, these aren't your woods. You've crossed over. You're in our land now.

"Do you really think you can ever escape? And what do you think will eat at you if you escape?"

He didn't want to hear anymore. He just wanted to get away from their madness. He took off running deeper and deeper into the woods. The trees grew even fatter, enormous, and even more crazily canted. As he ran, it felt like the forest was alive around him. He heard something like a heartbeat, felt the ground undulate beneath his feet. Behind him, he heard thirteen hot breaths, driving him deeper into the woods.

Fifty-two

The distance toward the road from where she stood in the pasture shouldn't have been that great but, with the increased weight in her stomach, Cassie didn't know if she could make it.

It wasn't just the weight in her stomach. It was everything. Everything felt like it was pressing down around her: the confusion, the fatigue, the fear, the whole big picture, whatever that was. Okay, the responsibility. That's what it was. She knew Elliot hadn't meant to, but he had instilled Cassie and John with a tremendous responsibility and, trudging along, Cassie was left to wonder if she had done the right thing. At the time, she thought she had, letting John take her there by the fire. She had thought it was the right thing because it had felt so very right but she knew from experience the things that feel the best often yield treacherous consequences. But what was done could not be undone. Sometimes, the only way out was through. That's what they had both done so far, muddled through, and it looked like that was exactly what they would have to continue doing.

It was impossibly dark. Neither the moon nor the stars afforded any light. And this only served to further wrap her confusion in more layers. How the hell was she supposed to figure out what to do if she couldn't see anything?

"Only the dead can leave."

The phrase ricocheted maddeningly around in her head. Why did she keep coming back to that? There had to be some importance to it. She couldn't help but think at least one answer to this insane mystery lay in that phrase.

Am I dead?

Is John dead?

Hell, she thought. *We both could've been dead the entire time.* It wouldn't have made a bit of difference. Together, they had accomplished exactly nothing. Alone, Cassie was a fearful, nervous wreck and John had racked up a smallish body count.

So what if they had been dead this entire time? Was it just some kind of fevered purgatory, each of them trying to reach some form of heaven? She had never thought about it like that. What if everyone, everything around them, all of the dead things, what if they were actually shadows of the living, carried into some kind of post-mortem subconscious?

She thought she was getting close to the wall.

She had to be getting close to the wall.

Just because it was dark, that didn't make space stretch any farther. What was a quarter of a mile in the daylight was still a quarter of a mile in the dark, wasn't it? Or was that just some other dismantling of logic this whole event was throwing at her?

She had begun to think of reaching the wall as a moment of truth. Living or dead?

If she passed through, she was dead, right? If she passed through, would she reach the other side, wandering into the heaven she hoped would house her after death? That would be the answer to life's greatest mystery, wouldn't it?

And if the wall contained her, if that imaginary or invisible wall blocked her passage, then the struggle continued, right? Then she would know she was still alive and there was still work to be done. But she didn't like what work she thought it was she might have to do. She felt the thing inside of her. She knew it had come from John and, deep down, she knew it was that thing that made John do all the things he had done. She thought she knew John, the real John, well enough to know he was not capable of doing those things unless something else was making him do them.

Alive or dead?

Alive or dead?

Alive or dead?

The wall was right in front of her. She felt the heavy current of energy pulse through her.

She would never find out.

She reached out, trying to plunge her hand into the invisible wall. Just as she felt that energy, squirming and alive, on her fingertips, flames jumped up in front of her, shooting out of the ground. She jumped back at the intense heat and dancing ferocity of the flames.

Now the flames were not just in front of her. They crackled out to either side of her, continuing to charge to the far perimeters of her vision, describing what she thought just had to be the perimeter of the Tantalus.

Great, she thought.

Sullenly, she walked back toward the pond. The heaviness squirmed around inside of her. The confusion and all the other bad feelings beat a tattoo on her exhausted and overworked brain.

She wondered what she was going to do next. The fire answered her question. Not only was it moving around the perimeter of the Tantalus, it was also thickening, creeping toward the middle of the Tantalus, consuming itself. How long would it take the fire to reach her?

Was this the Dark Fire?

She was ready to give up. It was bad enough having to fend off the Johnthing. Now she felt like she had the wrath of God to contend with also.

Fifty-three

With the Devils behind him, John reached the blackest part of the woods. The sick wet heat that sat on this area trapped him, making it hard to breathe or move. Frantic, he grabbed a tree, thinking he could climb it, anything to get away from those things, but his hands slid off. The tree was covered in a thick white mucous substance. He didn't think he wanted to know what it was. It clung to his hands, clammy and cold. He reached down to wipe it on his shorts, only remembering he was naked when his hands slicked his thighs with the substance.

And by the time his brain snapped into action, demanding that he *move*, it was too late.

He was trapped. His followers slowly encircled him, moving in closer. He had been in this situation before. The memories burned painfully in the front of his mind. He didn't know if he could stand to go through it again. If he could have, he would have killed himself just to ensure it didn't happen again.

They wanted to put another thing in him.

"Who *are* you people?" John asked.

"I think you already know. I offered you a service. You chose to accept it. But there was a price. You had to pay us by letting us use your body, but you broke the deal. We're the Devils. Every bad thing you've heard and your mommy was too afraid to tell you about. Didn't you like the way my mouth felt on your cock? Wasn't that what you wanted? It certainly felt like that was what you wanted. It is rare for someone so repulsed to be so aroused."

"I didn't know that would happen. I swear. You lied to me. You tricked me. You made me think it was all a dream."

"And did the girl trick you into fucking her?"

"How was I supposed to know that would happen? Why would I want Cassie to go through that?"

"You tell me. It seems like the safer of two situations."

"What do you mean?"

"You can be the hunter, or you can be the hunted. You put the thing in her and destroy her and our little stay here is over. The hunter. The hunted."

"So which are *you*?"

The woman fell silent. John continued.

"We found out some stuff on you. You're not invulnerable. Hell, I'm not even sure you exist. I don't even know if I'm alive."

The woman moved toward John and reached out a bony hand, placing it on his cheek. He recoiled at the touch.

"You're name's Ilya. Sorry about Ernst."

A flicker of something ran through Ilya's black eyes. "As much as you might search, you will never find out exactly what we are. We are on the far side of insanity. Those that have found out our true nature are totally gone by the time they find out. And those that know the truth—the ranters, the psychopathic, the insane— well, no one really listens to them, do they? And you haven't been quite right since your dear brother disappeared, have you? Maybe you *are* on your way to knowing. Maybe you *are* already on the far side of insanity."

And then she was gone. But the twelve men were still there, moving in closer and closer. He tried to run but was met with a wall of flesh. Hands reached out, taking him down to the ground, pushing his face into the rancid dirt. He recognized the smell. It was the same way the dead things around the pond smelled. Ripe and cloying and with some kind of thick substantiality so that breathing in the scent even though it was only a scent was more like breathing in some kind of heavy air that sat in his stomach, rising to tickle the back of his throat.

He couldn't move. He kicked out but his legs were being held. He thrashed. The more he thrashed, the more they tightened their grips. Then he felt them spread him. His breath rasped out of his throat to die in the dead dirt. His heart hammered in his chest. He felt it all the way in his head, threatening to rupture the veins and capillaries. He felt their cold dry touch move lasciviously up and down his skin. Bugs scurried beneath him. The way they scraped against his skin felt sinister.

He was aware of so many things.

He closed his eyes, praying to an abstract god.

It didn't help.

At first there was pain. A bright red flash of pain exploding in his head each time the given man jerked against his ass.

And then there was numbness until the man's cock fattened and shot his seed deep into John. More pain as he pulled it out. More pain as it was immediately replaced by another cock.

Waves of numbness and pain and never unconsciousness washed over him.

He wanted to scream but wondered what the point of that would be.

There wasn't any point. The screaming would only make the pain and the anger intensify. Grow. He needed to stay relatively calm and wait for a chance to get away from these things.

If he was still alive.

Do the dead have any worth?

What if he was dead?

If he was dead, could he still find some way to help undo this mess? To stop it from spreading?

If he was dead, would they be trying to create another sick child within him? And what about the first? If he was dead, could he find some way to stop it?

He counted the cocks that came inside him.

By the twelfth one, his whole body was numb. The tension snapped the muscles' stiff rigidity. It took all twelve of the monsters what it took one of the woman to do. There wasn't anything to do but wait for… what?

To wait for all hell to break loose.

Which is exactly what happened.

There was another boom, earth shattering, and he felt himself sliding, the earth crumbling away, the man on his back jerking with orgasm before separating from him. John turned and saw the robed figures looking toward him, from some place high above him. He saw them burst into flame. All at the same time. An instant flame that consumed them like dry paper.

I hope that's it, John thought. I hope they're finally fucking gone.

And he didn't care what was happening to him. He went with it, riding the dark invisible wave, speeding toward a black womb of unconsciousness.

Black.

Black.

Black.

Like death.

Like sleep.

Like mystery.

Fifty-four

Cassie slowly stepped back from the encroaching fire, toward the interior, cursing her dumb fate. For a moment, she thought about just charging on through it, to see if she could make it to the other side, but couldn't bring herself to do that. Instead, she just stared stupidly at it, slowly moving away from it, watching as it gradually came toward her.

And still, she wondered what the other side would be like.

You're dead anyway, right? It shouldn't make a bit of difference. What have you got to lose?

But, on the off chance she was still alive, which she was beginning to doubt more and more, there wasn't any way she could allow herself to feel the prick of those flames. She imagined getting to the other side and hitting the invisible wall, stuck there while the flames rolled over and through her.

What she had just gone through with John was different. That fire was different. She didn't know how to think of it, but it didn't seem particularly harmful. It was more like an ethereal cleansing, something that gave her renewed focus on their journey.

Maybe *it* was the Dark Fire.

Was John dead?

She didn't think so.

It was just another trick this place was playing on them. She realized now that's what it was. The entire time they had been here, it was just a series of tricks, one right after the other. In order to make the tricks stop, they had to find the person playing the tricks and make them stop. Cassie felt like John had a much better idea of who that might be than she did.

Right now the only thing she had to do was get past the most recent trick, that of the fire currently chasing her into the center of the field, licking hotly at her heels.

She broke out of her daze and ran for the pond because she thought that might be a safe haven. She hit a tree stump and went sprawling. The fire was spreading too incredibly fast now. Unnaturally fast. She stood up as quickly as possible and took off charging again, mentally feeling the pond's cool waters close around her skin.

When she reached the built-up bank of the pond, she could see a figure at its crest. Not really knowing what it could be, she kept a safe distance away. Once she also reached the top of the bank, she could tell from where she was that it was John, crumpled on the ground.

Or was it the Johnthing?

Cautiously, she crept over to the pile of flesh and bones.

No Johnthing.

Just John, curled up and looking completely out of it.

The fire ate up the grass between itself and the pond. Cassie heard its whooshing, hungry sound and grabbed John around the ankles.

"John, come on!"

Slowly, she backed into the pond, sliding John along behind her.

"Come on, John, wake up!" she said, hip deep in the pond.

The fire leapt to the crest of the pond's bank and, with a single giant lunge, she dragged John the rest of the way into the pond.

The water completely enclosed John and, Cassie didn't know if it was because he was drowning or if it was the chill from the water, but he sprang up and shouted, "Shit!"

She grabbed him around the shoulders.

"Look, John, we're in the pond. It was the only place to go. We're surrounded by fire. I think your whole farm is burning. Are you okay?"

"No," he said. "They put… they put another one of those things in me. And I don't think you're okay either. We probably need to be as far away from each other as possible."

"Jesus, John, this isn't good."

"You're damn right it's not good." This was punctuated with a giant thunderclap. Looking up, they saw lightning split through the sky, turning everything an electric blue.

They felt the waters in the pond churn over their skin. She remembered what John had told her about the pond on the night of the storm.

"What are we supposed to do?"

"I don't think we really have much of a choice."

She felt his hot breath on her cheek, his wet nose pressed against her wet ear.

"I think we just have to go with it," he said.

"But where does it go?"

"Your guess is every bit as good as mine. Probably someplace bad. I think this is where they came from."

"I don't want to go there. Elliot said if we went there and the Tantalus closed on us, then we would be stuck there forever."

"I think I was already there."

The pond's churning became more violent, swirling over them, emptying itself into some hidden chasm and spiraling down into the earth. John pulled Cassie into him, her back pressed up against his chest, and they both stared ahead as the reverse waterspout carried them down.

Fifty-five

Somewhere along the way, they became separated.

Sensations swirled through Cassie. She felt the slimy, silty mud of the pond and the pond's water enter her through every orifice, surging through her veins, becoming her blood. She was afraid to open her eyes. From all around her she heard some type of wet snarl and, to stop her from envisioning anything worse, she imagined some huge bathtub drain, all that water and mud being sucked through it. She figured she would be sucked through as well.

The snarl grew louder and louder, beating against the back of her brain. She was powerless. She wanted to remain powerless. What was the sense in trying? What had trying got them so far?

It had brought them here. And here felt like the bottom of the earth. She was beginning to wonder if here was hell although she didn't know if anything could rival the hell she had felt for the past several days where every second, every minute, every hour was a struggle with life itself.

The snarl was deafening.

She felt herself plummeting faster and faster. She made one last attempt to fling her arms and legs around, hoping to feel John, and came up with nothing.

It looked like it was finally time to walk alone.

She felt something squeezing her. She tried to open her eyes and they were just as quickly mucked over, her eyeballs burning, forcing her lids closed and tears to well up to the surface to try and remove the debris. The second her eyes were open brought her nothing. Not a vision closer to understanding what was going on around her. The snarl vibrated through her viscera and she thought she must finally be in the place where all that muck and water converged. She closed her eyes, tensed her muscles, and waited, even though she was sick and tired of waiting.

She had done far too much waiting the past few days.

But the waiting was almost over.

Fifty-six

The only thing John could think about was Cassie.

(*Cassie Cassie Cassie CASSIE!*)

And she was nowhere to be found. Searching frantically, he groped for her in the mess surrounding him and came up with nothing.

How could she get so far away in such a short time?

He didn't even remember letting go of her. It was more like she had somehow been plucked silently from his protective grasp. He still couldn't shake the feeling he was somehow responsible for all this.

Dropping.

Dropping through the earth and completely unable to stop himself, he didn't imagine a giant drain. He saw that horrible woman. His eyes were closed and all of this was in his head. That horrible woman. In front of him. She was huge. As big as the cosmos. Her gray and tattered rotting skin spread out in all directions, her legs open to the waterspout, to John. He saw her gaping vagina, hanging in sick folds, beckoning him like a vacuum. As he got closer he smelled death. It was a sickening smell, old and meaty, scraping at the back of his throat.

And as he drew even closer, something else happened.

The woman was disintegrating.

And screaming.

The sounds of her screams soothed John. He could listen to them as long as possible. They seemed to calm his frayed nerves, run a relaxing hand along his brain.

Intently, he turned his mind's eye on the woman, unable to look away.

Her skin peeled away from the bone, floated off into space, her vagina crumbling and dropping away. Her black blood flowed from her skeleton, disappearing in the space below. And he was left with the skeleton itself, yellow-black bones separating from themselves, spinning around a blue circular opening in front of him.

With a final screech, the woman's bones exploded a fiery red and John shot through the opening, into blackness.

Fifty-seven

Cassie emerged in a foreign place. A low valley with an abandoned house sitting atop a small hill in the middle. Hills rose up around the small valley, excluding the world around it.

She sniffed the air around her. It smelled fresh and new. There was rain in the air although it wasn't coming down at the moment. The first rays of the sun were breaking over the hill in front of her. She felt like she should hurry but, since she had no idea where she was, she didn't see the point in hurrying. She stood still for a few minutes, breathing the air and watching the sun brighten the sky.

For a moment, she thought she felt good.

Then she remembered the thing inside of her.

The panic she had become so familiar with was back upon her.

The rain came down and she walked to the sanctity and shelter of the large house on the top of the small hill. She crept up the decrepit stairs to a room on the second floor and, as dawn broke over the hills, she curled up on the dusty plank wood floor and fell asleep.

<h1 style="text-align:center">Fifty-eight</h1>

Even the mellow light of the blue dawn seemed harsh on John's eyes. Looking around, he didn't see what he expected to see. He didn't know exactly what he *did* expect to see. Maybe something that fit more comfortably into the fabric of the last week: conflagrations, explosions... a mass grave, maybe. Instead he had been granted this bucolic valley, green hills poking up all around it, an old farmhouse sitting grimly in the middle.

He took a deep breath, letting the cool moisture of this new air into his lungs. It felt fresh and clean, unlike the sweltering stagnancy of the other area. He didn't figure it mattered where they were. He didn't care, just so long as it wasn't there.

He wasn't at all afraid of Cassie. He supposed they had, in a sense, discovered the nature of the beast. It was dawn now, she couldn't hurt him. Besides, she had stuck by him the entire time, not that that time was over now. He still had another one of those things growing inside of him, it just hadn't had the chance to be subjected to the darkness as of yet.

He began walking up the small hill to the house at the top. There was something sinister about the house but he couldn't let it bother him. There was something about the peculiar cant of it, something that made it seem as though it were leaning toward him. The way the hollowed out upper windows were bent made him think of those occasional people you see on the street, those people who will make eye contact with you until you have passed them, and after you pass them you get a shiver down your spine for no other reason than what that look in their eyes contained. Hard to explain, but that's what looking at this house made him think of.

He walked up the five steps and brought himself onto the sagging, rotted porch. The musty, damp smell of the wood made him think of antique shops and old bookstores. The barn back home. He didn't find it at all displeasing. If anything, it seemed inviting.

Careful where he put his feet, he entered the house. The only thing on the first floor was an old blue couch sitting catty-corner in the far right side of the room. It was an old Victorian-style couch. The blue was of a hue he didn't really think of when he thought about old furniture, which he didn't do very much. He thought of it as electric blue. The fabric was something that begged to be touched. He ran his fingers along it. It wasn't leather even though, from a distance, it looked like it could have been. It was cracked in places, brown dust covered the tip of his finger when he brought it away. Maybe someone had it reupholstered, he thought. Maybe it was aged satin.

"Cassie!" he called.

No answer.

"Cassie!" he tried again.

He walked into the back of the house, divided up into two more rooms.

Nobody there.

He turned to his right and started up the staircase, avoiding the two or three steps that had gone black with damp rot. At the top of the stairs, he saw Cassie, covered in blood and curled up below the window.

He put a hand on her bony shoulder and gently shook her.

"Cassie," he whispered in her ear. "Cassie?"

Groggily, she opened her eyes. "Huh?"

"You were sleeping."

"So tired."

"I know but… I think we're almost at the end. I think we have a long day in front of us." He hated the thought of there being an end to this, as crazy as that was. It had occurred to him that, when this was over, he would probably never see Cassie again. If they were both still alive, which he doubted, and if they both emerged with their minds intact, he couldn't see why she would ever want to see him again. It would just bring it all back to her. He couldn't imagine anyone wishing that upon themselves.

"I'm going to go downstairs," he told her. "Will you be down in a few minutes?"

"Yeah," she said, staring dreamily at the sunlight streaming in through the window.

He ran his hand down her arm, stood up and headed back down the stairs.

Fifty-nine

He went out to the porch and sat down on the top step. The dawn was beautiful, all red and gold, smeared across the sky. He thought about what he was getting ready to propose to Cassie and it sent a shiver down his spine. A shiver that hit his stomach and bloomed into nausea.

He heard the porch creak as she stepped out onto it. He turned to look at her over his shoulder. He noticed the slight protuberance of her belly, speckles of blood on her thighs. She came toward him and sat down beside him.

"Rough night, huh?"

She tried her best to laugh.

"Do you think we're still alive?" he asked.

She didn't answer right away. He heard her breathe in a shaky breath.

"Yes," she said finally.

"Why?"

"Because, if we weren't, we wouldn't have these things inside of us."

"You know what we have to do, right?"

"Fraid so."

"And then what?"

"And then we should find some clothes."

And then John did laugh. It seemed like such a banal suggestion he couldn't help but appreciate it.

"That would probably be a good idea," he said.

"I don't know," she said, serious again. "I guess we try and find our way back. Where do you think we are?"

"I don't know. Could be just about anywhere, I guess." He paused, took a breath, said, "Actually, I think this is the Sad House."

"From the book?"

He nodded.

"I need to see my parents. I need to see my friends. What about you? I mean, do you have any friends?"

"Actually, I don't. I might just stay right here. Seems as good a place as any."

"Maybe my parents would let you stay with us for a bit. You know, until you get back on your feet."

"That would probably be awkward."

"What do you mean?"

"Do you really think you'll want anything to do with me when this is all over?"

"Do you really think I'm like that, John?"

"No, that's not what I meant. I mean, supposing we actually get through everything okay and we do get back home, won't it bring back a bunch of things you don't want to remember just by looking at me."

"John, if we get through this, I'll wear you like a symbol of triumph."

He put his arm around her and pulled her close to him, leaning his head against the top of hers.

"I know this sounds crazy," he said. "But I've gotten closer to you than I've ever been to anyone."

"I feel the same way," she said. "You wanna get this over with?"

"I think that might be best. Who should go first?"

"Well, I was thinking yours would probably be the easiest. Maybe you should go first. You wanna go inside?"

"Not really. But I guess we should."

They walked back into the house, into its musty gloom.

"Have you thought about how you're going to do this?" he asked.

"Yeah, I have. Why don't you sit down on that couch."

He moved over to the couch and sat down. What she seemed prepared to do had crossed his mind but he had dismissed it.

She got down on her knees between his legs.

"You know this could be dangerous for you," he said. "I could probably just jerk off."

"I thought about that too. But, this is what I figure: the thing that's inside of you, okay, it will probably only leave if it thinks it can enter another human host, like when we had sex."

"That sounds reasonable."

"I mean, if you jerk off and nothing happens, then we might have lost the chance, you know. I know you're young but... We don't want to have to go up in you."

He shivered at the thought and then said, "You know, I'm sorry this all happened."

"You need to stop saying that. There isn't a damn thing that has happened that has been your fault. We're innocents in this, John. Remember that."

He still wasn't too sure about that, but it was nice to know she felt that way. If they lived past the next few hours, he didn't think he would ever be able to shake away the guilt of the past week.

She lifted his penis up by the head, laying it against his lower stomach. She ran her tongue up its flaccid length, enclosed her mouth around it. The only thing he could think about was the pain that was going to end this session. She put a hand beneath his scrotum and gently sucked him.

Nothing.

She stopped and looked at him.

"You can't think about the pain."

"Jesus, it's still sore as hell from yesterday."

"Look at it this way. If you make it through this, imagine all the exquisite head you can have when it's all over. Besides, it shouldn't hurt nearly as much as it did yesterday. I figure these things must double in size about every day. I'm guessing it's relatively small. You're already broke in." She laughed.

"I guess maybe I'm kind of nervous, too."

"We have to do this. Are you going to let me suck your dick now?"

"Yes."

"Are you going to get hard?"

"Yes."

"You can watch me if that makes it better. Or think about whatever you want. Whoever you want. Do you want to watch me suck you, John?"

"Yes."

What she was doing was already working. She encircled a hand around the base and leaned back over him, pulling her mouth up and moving her hand down. He gripped the couch, watching her head bob up and down. She opened her eyes and met his and that was it. He felt it. First the intense pleasure and then…

The pain ran screaming from his cock. He tried to pull her head away from him but she knocked his hands away. Then, all of a sudden, she yanked her mouth off of him and went coughing back into the other room, her eyes rolling up into the back of her head.

He got behind her and tried to perform the Heimlich. She stuck her fingers down her throat and he felt her diaphragm spasm as she threw up all over the floor. The vomit was red and somewhere in the middle of it was a white, marble-sized thing that moved rapidly through it. John leaned over it and stomped it with his heel. Repeatedly. He brought his foot up and brought it back down, hearing the satisfying crunch of the creature and the sick warm splatter of vomit flecking against his calves.

Cassie lay on the floor, exhausted. John went over to her and lay next to her, putting his arm across her chest.

"One down," she said, laughing through ravaged vocal cords.

"Should we rest?"

"Might as well just push on."

"Are you scared?"

"No more than you."

"I mean, I saw what that thing did when it went into you and it *wanted* to do that. I'm afraid of what it will do if it doesn't want to come out."

"Can't think about that."

She stood up and crossed over to the couch. She sat back on it, pale and sweaty, puke slathered all down the front of her body.

"I just want to get this whole mess over with," she said. She didn't necessarily think she believed in God, but there was a part of her that wondered if this was punishment for going through with her abortion.

John stood up and crossed over to her.

"How do I…?"

"Well, I think you're just going to have to reach up there."

"Won't that hurt?"

"Yes, John, it will hurt. But hopefully it will be the last time I hurt for a long time. I'm tired of hurting. This will get the hurting over with. Besides, you're forgetting, I'm a girl. I've been to the gynecologist. I'm used to being probed. Do you want to get this over with or not? I know it's not very sexy, but shooting demons out of your dick isn't too hot either."

"I guess you have a point there."

"We're almost finished. I can feel it. Come on."

He crouched down. He didn't want to get down on his knees because he thought that would relinquish too much control. He felt like they would probably have more problems with this one than the last one. He folded his fingers together so they formed a singular cone and slowly slid them in between Cassie's labia, still moist with yesterday's blood.

"Do it fast. I don't know what this thing will do if it figures out you're coming after it. I don't want it tearing through my stomach or anything like that."

As quickly as he could, he pushed inward until his whole hand was in Cassie. She sucked in air through her teeth, all of her muscles tightening. He felt her sex clamp down on his wrist. He continued to push his hand deeper.

"Grab the first thing you come to," she gasped.

His fingertips brushed along something. He opened his hand to close it around the object. Cassie winced, lifted her buttocks off the couch. Quickly, he closed his hand around the object and brought it out of her.

He had the thing by the legs. It made a hissing sound as it thrashed around. Cassie was unable to help him. She had slid off the couch and was now lying doubled up on the floor.

The thing swung its head up and gnashed at John's forearm, taking a hunk with it. A hideous baby with fangs.

John brought his arm back and threw the thing against the far wall. It made a solid thud and landed on the floor. John had already crossed the room over to the thing, expecting it to try and scurry away. Instead, it stood up. Unfolded, it was no more than a foot high. John still found himself slightly afraid of it. He thought about the stair that he had pried loose, lying abandoned over there by the couch.

The thing bared its teeth and launched itself at him, going for his neck. He ducked and the thing went flying over his head, regaining its balance and throwing itself between Cassie's legs. She moaned and tried to roll over where her opening wasn't exposed.

John bounded over to the creature and grabbed it by its feet, slinging it head first into the floor while still holding onto its feet. The blow managed to daze it long enough for John to grab the board.

With all of the energy he had left, he threw the thing against the floor. It lay stunned and John lined the board up with its neck, holding it with both hands so the narrow side would come down on it.

He brought the board down, relishing the satisfying crunch it made as it snapped through the thing's spinal column. He continued to bring the board down until the head separated from the body, leaving mangled folds of skin where they had once been connected.

He didn't know why he did what he did next. He was filled with hate and dread and exhaustion. He got down on his knees and rolled the thing over on its back. He slipped his fingers into the loose skin at its neck and tore its tender flesh apart. Once he had the thing split to the waist, he reached in under the rib cage until he felt what must have been the thing's tiny heart. Wrapping his thumb and first two fingers around it, he yanked it out. It made a sound like chicken being separated from the bone and John popped it into his mouth.

The taste of the blood made him want to gag as he chomped at the muscle, making sure it was shredded, tattered, drained of its vital fluids. And then he swallowed it.

Sixty

He crossed to where Cassie lay on the floor. He looked down at her. She cried. Her hands were tucked between her legs. He didn't think she was crying from pain. Something else, maybe.

"We're not finished yet, are we?"

"I'm afraid not."

"Can you go alone?"

"I really think we should go together."

He offered a hand to help her up. She took it and stood shakily.

"So we...?" she said.

"We need to go downstairs. If there is a downstairs."

"And that's where you think it'll be?"

"And maybe her."

"We have nothing."

"Only ourselves."

"Terrible idea."

John picked up the remains of the fetuses and held them cupped in his hands."

"What are you doing?"

"If the Dark Fire's down there, we're going to discard these in it."

Sixty-one

John followed the description he remembered from the book.

He opened the door and saw a set of stone stairs leading down. Just like in the book. Maybe Cassie was right. It felt suicidal doing this without anything.

He opened the door at the bottom of the stairway. There was the large table in a room of bluish light. No one sat at the table. John felt a weird moment where the present overlapped what had happened in the book. Why hadn't they held onto the book? It had probably burned up in the fire.

There was a door on the other side of the room. If everything John thought was true, the Low Church would be on the other side of that door. And the Dark Fire would be burning inside. What he could do with that knowledge, he had no idea.

"Through there?" Cassie asked.

John nodded.

"Let's do it."

Cassie opened the door.

"Try to avoid looking into the fire if it's there. And if I happen to disappear into it, try to pull me out."

John walked in first.

The Church lay before him. There would be yet another door

that led to the Dark Fire. He figured if Ilya were there, she would try to prevent him from opening that door.

He didn't see her in the Church.

They walked through the silent church, corpses hanging from the walls like sconces.

John pulled the next door open.

He heard the fire blazing from within before he saw it.

He felt a hand grip his arm and yank him toward the fire.

Sixty-two

And into the fire.

Much like the fire beside the pond, this one didn't destroy. With this one he felt no burning or pain at all.

John held out the pulp in his hands and said, "Your children."

Ilya made no attempt to take them.

John let them drop to the floor. He tried his hardest to focus on Ilya's black eyes so he couldn't see any of the fire blazing around him. But he thought he saw plenty of it reflected in her eyes. Maybe the Dark Fire came from within her.

John noticed something.

"Where are your monsters?" Their absence made John think this was more his turf than Ilya's. He couldn't rationalize it.

"I don't need them. I already have you here. In the Dark Fire. It's working on you. You won't be able to resist it."

"And then? What? I'm not special."

"But you are," she said.

"You can't leave. You're trapped."

She smiled. He noticed she looked into his eyes as intently as he looked into hers.

"I saw what you really are. And I saw that thing destroyed."

"You will never see what I really am."

There was movement from behind her. John flicked his eyes away just long enough for her to catch the movement. She leapt toward him, coming at his face with her claws. A man sprang up behind her and knocked her off course, driving her into the ground.

"Elliot!" John shouted.

"Run back out," Elliot said. "Get out of here!"

John hesitated.

Ilya now unleashed a vicious chant.

John began backing away from them. Toward where he had entered the fire, he hoped.

Elliot shouted, "Your body has been destroyed! Your body has been destroyed!"

Then John saw Elliot's body disintegrate like he'd seen the woman's and then he was outside of the Fire, trying to look away.

He rolled onto his back and saw Cassie in front of him. Above her, on the ceiling, he saw something that looked like a small swirling cloud and then it was gone.

A boom exploded through the Low Church.

He saw Cassie bathed in a holocaustic light and then everything went black.

Sixty-three

They found consciousness at the same time. They were back in John's field but it didn't look anything like what it looked like before. The whole area was charred, the ground black with the occasional orange of a glowing cinder. Once awake, they stood up quickly because the ash was burning their backs.

The whole area was devoid of anything except the black ash.

"Wow," Cassie said.

"Yeah," John said. "Are we alive?"

"Don't know."

"Do you care?"

"Not really."

"Me either. Look." He pointed west.

A large black storm front approached them, the clouds swirling back on themselves. He let the moist, cool wind run over his naked body.

"This is the one that will clean everything," he said. "We have to stay out in it. It needs to put us back together."

"Yes," Cassie said. She crossed over to John and they embraced. He felt her small breasts press against his chest, felt her breathing against him, the heat that came out of her mouth. In that instant, he knew it was an impossibility they were dead. Death could not be like this. He couldn't fathom any pleasure in death and he was holding every pleasure he'd ever wanted in his arms right now.

The rain came down softly at first.

He had his head resting on the top of Cassie's head, tears rolling out of his shut eyes.

"Look," Cassie said.

He opened his eyes and blinked the tears away. The rain fell to the ground, hissing and sending up tendrils of steam. Here and there, through the black ash, he saw shoots of green growing up from the ash. It reminded him of the time-lapse films he had to watch in biology.

The harder the rain came, the faster everything grew.

A half hour later, when the big storm actually hit, John and Cassie were wandering through a sort of paradise. Together, they walked down toward the road, toward that invisible line.

Thunder roared through the sky.

"Are we dead, John? Are we dead?" Cassie asked as they stepped into the invisible wall.

Unrestrained, they came out the other side.

John looked at Cassie, looked her up and down, looked at all of her rain cleansed skin.

"No, we're not dead, Cassie. But the nightmare is."

Together, naked, they circled one another around the storm darkened country road.

"It's not over yet," John said.

"Oh, shit, what the fuck are you talking about?"

They continued to circle around one another.

"Does it feel over to you?"

"No, but, I want to go home, John boy."

"We'll get there, eventually. Why are you in such a hurry?"

"What are you talking about, crazy boy?"

"I think we need to take shelter from the storm."

As they circled, Cassie continued to stare at John, hungry for answers.

"What about we take shelter in the shade?"

"But everything burned."

"And everything's coming back."

"You've become cryptic in your old age."

"Follow me."

John stopped circling and ran up the driveway. It should have been impossible to follow him, but Cassie managed, keeping pace with him, nipping at his heels.

They were up around the house, now a pile of blackened rocks. The cars in the driveway were hollowed-out blackened shells. In the backyard stood the gargantuan oak tree. It was also charred, all of its limbs gone. But it was still tall, the tallest thing in the yard. The rain beat down around them, the thunder rolling over them.

"You're insane, Fresk. I'm not standing under that thing."

"I don't want to stand under it. I just want to look at it."

"Well, there it is."

As soon as she said that, a massive bolt of lightning shot down and struck the tree, six feet from the bottom. The top portion fell slowly away from them, crashing into the now lush green grass of the yard.

John approached the tree, reaching out toward it, pulling away the bark.

"Help me with this," he said.

She approached the tree and began stripping the rotten wood. Together, they pulled away a huge chunk of the trunk and, inside the tree, curled into a ball, was a man. Elliot.

Elliot uncurled himself and stood up in the tree. Cautiously, he stepped out.

"Is this…" he said, looking around.

"This is home," John said.

"There've been a few changes."

"To say the least."

Then John and Elliot embraced. Cassie wept at the sight,

oblivious to the storm around them.

"So," Elliot said. "Did people stop wearing clothes while I was away?"

"We have some things to tell you."

"Guys? Do you think we could talk about them at my house?"

"Maybe there's no need," Elliot said.

They turned to look as the pile of rocks lifted themselves and slowly formed back into the house Cassie had never seen.

"I can't go in there," she said.

And there was a temporary silence as Cassie turned and walked toward the road. Elliot and John followed her as she led the way into the town of Lynchville.

Conclusion

It was midnight at the Wake Up Screaming Café. Two months had passed. The three of them sat in a corner booth, John and Cassie on one side, Elliot on the other. Beside Elliot sat a knapsack. They all sipped at their coffee. They had been there for the past three hours.

"I'm glad you guys told me everything," Elliot said.

"We wouldn't be here if it wasn't for you," Cassie said.

Elliot waved her away as if what she'd said was ridiculous. "You seem perfect for John. You need to stay together, no matter what kind of shit life decides to throw at you."

"Maybe, one day, you can tell us what happened to you in the twelve years you've been gone," John said.

"Hopefully. I'm not really sure I know, at this point."

"Is that why you're leaving?"

"Sure, that's part of it. I can't really stay in Lynchville for the rest of my life. There's a whole world I haven't seen out there. And there are places where our world overlaps that other world."

"The world you *have* seen."

Elliot nodded.

"And you want to go back to that world, don't you?" John

asked.

"Well, I don't know if I'm in that big of a hurry."

"I guess I just don't really understand."

"I guess I couldn't expect you to. One day, hell, one week or month maybe, we'll sit down and I'll tell you everything I know. But look, Mom and Dad are gone. Me and you, space and time can't separate us. We'll always have each other. I just need some time to think and explore so this all makes a little bit more sense for each of us."

"Are you going to look for her?" Cassie asked.

"Who? Ilya?"

"Yeah."

"Well, I don't really know if I have to look for her. I think she might find me. Or somebody like her. I'm not sure that revenge is really in my blood. They found me once and they took me but I got away. They found me again and almost destroyed you and John because of that."

"I think you lost me," John said.

"They wanted me to do things for them. I refused. I can't tell you what those things are because you wouldn't understand right now."

"You have to do what you have to do," John said. "You'll let us know when you find what it is you're looking for."

"You'll be the first to know."

Elliot grabbed his knapsack and stood up.

"I don't want to miss the bus," he said.

John stood up and hugged him. Elliot reached across the table and shook Cassie's hand. He slung the knapsack over his shoulder and headed for the door. John slid back into the booth and grabbed Cassie's hand. He raked her hair back behind her ear and said, "Well, it looks like it's just me and you again."

"Uh oh," Cassie said. "That could be trouble."

Wayne Hixon lives in Illinois. This is his second novel. Contact him at wayne66hixon@yahoo.com.

Other Grindhouse Press Titles

#007 – *Hi I'm a Social Disease: Horror Stories* by Andersen Prunty

#006 – *A Life On Fire* by Chris Bowsman

#005 – *The Sorrow King* by Andersen Prunty

#004 – *The Brothers Crunk* by William Pauley III

#003 – *The Horribles* by Nathaniel Lambert

#002 – *Vampires in Devil Town* by Wayne Hixon

#001 – *House of Fallen Trees* by Gina Ranalli

#000 – *Morning is Dead* by Andersen Prunty